# Ready

# To

# Fall

6/13/00

For Cathy,

Enjoy!! Especeally

the Swim mom stuff!

With all best,

Claire

# Ready

# To

# Fall

a novel

*Claire Cook*

## Claire Cook

Bridge Works Publishing Company
Bridgehampton, New York

Published in the United States by Bridge Works Publishing
Company, Bridgehampton, New York. Distributed in the United
States by National Book Network, Lanham, Maryland.

For descriptions of this and other Bridge Works books visit the
Web site of National Book Network at www.nbnbooks.com.

FIRST EDITION

The characters and events in this book are fictitious. Any similarity
to actual persons, living or dead, is coincidental and not intended
by the author.

*Library of Congress Cataloging-in-Publication Data*

Cook, Claire
    Ready to fall : a novel / Claire Cook.—1st ed.
      p.  cm.
    ISBN 1-882593-32-4 (alk. paper)
    1. Middle aged women—New England—Fiction.
2. Neighborhood—New England—Fiction.
3. Electronic mail messages—Fiction.  I. Title.

  PS3553.O55317 R4 2000
  813'.54—dc21                           99-055389

10  9  8  7  6  5  4  3  2  1

Jacket design/illustration by Eva Auchincloss
Book design by Eva Auchincloss

Printed in the United States of America

In memory of my mother,
Margaret Gibson Cook

Thanks to everyone who offered support and encouragement, especially Barbara Browne, Gary Davidson, Dayle Dickinson, Wendy Nelson, and Holly Whelan.

Eternal thanks to my writing group—Elizabeth Berg, Betsy Coonley, Helen Fremont, Alex Johnson, Kate Kruschwitz, and Mary Mitchell—for teaching me as much about kindness and honesty as about writing from the heart.

Many thanks to my husband, Jake Jacobucci, our daughter, Garet, and our son, Kaden, for the time and space to write.

# Part 1

Date: Friday, June 5, 1:03 P.M. EDT
From: SwimSlave
To: Wanderlust
Subj: Apology to Thomas Marsh from Beth Riordan

Thank goodness! I found your e-mail address on the back of your lovely travel book, *Walden Pond and Its Environs: The Transcendentalist's Tour.* I am writing to apologize again for this morning's incident at the library. I assure you that it was quite by accident that your book made it into the stack I was dropping off at the library's "Take It or Leave It" pile.

As I explained during our brief encounter, I had spent the morning weeding out my children's bookshelves, deciding that *Charlotte's Web* could stay but *Goosebumps* would have to go, that sort of thing. I hadn't even attempted to thin out my own collection, other than to grab a couple of paperback novels I was sure I'd never look at again. I must also add that I was only contemplating fiction this morning, which should be further proof that discarding your guidebook was an honest mistake.

And what an awful coincidence that you should happen by at the very moment I was abandoning your book. I was so humiliated when you picked it up, wrote *Best Wishes, Thomas Marsh* with an elegant flourish, and handed it back to me. If that wasn't enough to make me suffer from terminal embarrassment, I discovered you were the same Thomas Marsh who lives next door. And I'd always thought you were in sales.

I don't mean to pressure you, but unless I am sure you have forgiven me, I will find it difficult to leave my house for fear of running into you. By the way, I reread your entire book the moment I got home from the library. I must say it was even better the second time around. During my original reading I may have been too focused on planning a family outing to fully appreciate its scope. I particularly like Thoreau's statement about how he put a piece of paper under his pillow so that he could write in the dark if he couldn't sleep, and the way you tied it in with the suggestion that the reader consider keeping a travel journal.

I hope this e-mail finds you since I'm not sure I'd have the nerve to seek you out in person. I don't think I ever quite believe that e-mail will actually get to its intended recipient, but that might be because I haven't been online for very long. That is the appropriate expression, isn't it? I always want to say *in*line, but then I remember that inline is for skates and supermarkets.

Well, Thomas, I'll bet you're in the middle of writing another wonderful book, so I won't keep you.

Here goes. I'm going to push *Send* now.

Date:    Friday, June 5, 1:10 P.M. EDT
From:   SwimSlave
To:       Wanderlust
Subj:   Thank you

Thank you for getting back to me so quickly. I did half expect you to simply open your window, stick your head out, and yell, "I forgive you, Beth!" across our yards.

Oh, and it was sweet of you to tell me that my e-mail was perfectly sent and that I have "the makings of techno talent". Not even close to being true, but nice to hear anyway. Sometimes I wonder how it is that I live in a house bursting with computers and yet have managed to stay so functionally illiterate. It seems that my family moved into the computer world and I was left behind licking my stamps.

You see, my children meet their friends in private cyber rooms to talk in fancy fonts and brilliantly colored words. They send each other mysterious communications they refer to as IMs, which I eventually came to understand simply means "Instant Messages", although it sounds far more menacing. My husband, Pete, spends his workday surrounded by the trappings of this new world. Each day he comes home from work I understand him less, not that he ever suggests bringing me up-to-date. If you asked me what his company does, I would have to say that all I really know is at one time they invented a kind of improved track for the ball of the computer mouse to roll around in. It seems, if you turn your mouse upside down and unscrew its underside (something I admit I couldn't bring myself to do), there is a free-rolling ball inside that must be guided but not inhibited by a collection of tiny metal strips. Apparently Pete's company improved the existing technology with just the right combination of slip and grip so that the mouse could more efficiently escort that tiny little arrow around the computer screen. That was several years ago, and probably the last computer development I understood in any real depth.

Well, enough about me. Again, I greatly appreciate your forgiveness, and I thank you for upgrading my techno self-image.

Oh, I almost forgot. I was so sorry to hear about your marital troubles. I'm glad you felt you could talk to me about them and that you could even ask me for a favor. Of course I'll help you out. I'm always happy to help a neighbor, especially one who has forgiven me for my completely unintentional insult.

Date: Friday, June 5, 10:12 P.M. EDT
From: SwimSlave
To:     Wanderlust
Subj:   Quick Question

This is absolutely none of my business but do you have any idea *why* your wife left you? Feel free not to answer that, Thomas. And let me assure you that, whatever your answer, *should* you decide to answer, I will still be happy to keep an eye on your house whenever you travel.

I guess I've just been wondering lately about relationships. Exactly how happy should one expect to be at this stage of one's life?

Date: Friday, June 5, 11:25 P.M. EDT
From: SwimSlave
To:     Wanderlust
Subj:   What a Nice Surprise

I didn't think you'd be awake and reading your mail so late at night, and I certainly didn't expect you to answer so promptly. But, what you said about relationships— that "everything has a shelf life, be it marriage or brussels sprouts". Do you really think that's true? Do you think there's an expiration date stamped on some out-of-the-way corner of every marriage?

Date:    Saturday, June 6, 9:02 A.M. EDT
From:    SwimSlave
To:      Wanderlust
Subj:    Your Opinion, Please

Do you have a minute, Thomas? Pete has taken the girls to swim practice, our son P.J. is watching cartoons, and I really could use someone to talk to. I did try to talk to my husband earlier but that wasn't exactly a resounding success. I got up this morning when he did, even though technically it's my morning to sleep in, put on a pot of coffee and brought in the paper while he was taking a shower. I even made blueberry pancakes.

"Pete," I said, before the kids came downstairs. "I'm sorry I've been so grouchy lately. Maybe we should try to talk about it. Because it seems to me as if everything is about someone else. Either you or the kids or the house. I feel as if the only time anyone even talks to me is to complain or criticize or to place an order for something they need."

"Uh-hmm."

"Uh-hmm? That's all you have to say—uh-hmm?"

And my husband of almost two decades put down his fork and looked at me over his reading glasses. He took off his glasses, placed them on the newspaper beside

8

his plate and said, "I think I'm getting conjunctivitis in my right eye."

Answer me this, Thomas, if I'm not too presumptuous. Does it sound to you like Pete and I are having marital problems, and, if so, how do they compare with yours?

Date:    Saturday, June 6, 10:37 A.M. EDT
From:   SwimSlave
To:      Wanderlust
Subj:   Seriously?

I can't believe you once forgot your wife's name when you were introducing her to someone. That's *really* bad, Thomas. Thank you for making me laugh, whether or not it's actually true or you made it up just to make me feel better.

Date:    Sunday, June 7, 12:03 P.M. EDT
From:   SwimSlave
To:      Wanderlust
Subj:   Quick Note

Pete and I will be leaving soon to pick up the kids from their overnight at his parents' house. I'm glad I have last night to think about because my day will consist of Pete's mother's overcooked roast and the recirculated comments about the sorry state of the world that pass for conversation with my in-laws. I'm sure I could transcribe the whole visit in advance right now, and when

I return tonight to check my work, I might be off by only three or four sentences.

Let me just say, before I rush off, how happy I was to run into you in the dark last night. Pete and I were having an impromptu cookout, an idea he came up with on the way home from his parents' house. "So, honey, how about having a few people over tonight?" he asked in a voice that was a little too cheery. Lately we both jump to fill our house back up whenever it empties of kids.

I said "yes" to the cookout just as cheerily, looking over at Pete as he was driving. Pete has the kind of looks that make him seem less substantial as the years go by. His hair is turning pale instead of grey, his skin is somehow lighter. He's getting shorter, I think, as if gravity were pulling his tall lanky body closer to the ground. I felt a burst of sympathy for him, until it occurred to me that he's probably aging better than I am.

When we got home, Pete made some phone calls while I dashed out to the store. And the cookout was fine, if predictable. All of the guests stayed outside until the mosquitoes chased them home or into the shelter of our screened porch. I had just wandered back outside to see if there were any stray napkins or paper plates that needed to be picked up. And there you were, standing at the junction of our yards. Even with that salt-and-pepper hair and mustache, in the dark you looked almost like a teenager. Maybe it was the wrinkled T-shirt you wore with your jeans, or the fact that you're in amazingly good shape for a man who must be . . . how old?

Pete is downstairs yelling for me. Bye for now.

Date:  Sunday, June 7, 7:26 P.M. EDT
From:  SwimSlave
To:    Wanderlust
Subj:  Continued

I'm back and do you know what I wondered about all day? I know you're always traveling, but how is it that we've lived next to each other for years and years and never even had a real conversation? Is it a New England thing or something that only happens in certain suburbs of Boston, this studious ignoring of one's neighbors? Or is neighborliness a dying convention, like attending town meetings and taking trash to the dump?

How many years have we casually avoided each other? If I passed your driveway to pull into my own while you were standing in your yard, you would look up at the trees as if you had just noticed an unusual bird, maybe the yellowest oriole or even a lost tern that had wandered inland. Or you might squat down to the shrubbery as if you were inspecting for mites or rust or whatever rhododendrons are likely to catch.

It went both ways. If I drove in, my daughters in the car, returning from the morning swim practice, not quite 8 A.M. and I'd been out for over three hours already, I might pass you heading out for another one of your trips. If we couldn't avoid a wave, it was done without eye contact and with only the most superficial of smiles. Imagine sharing a small road, and each of us acting as if the other didn't exist.

I think somewhere along the line we had decided not to like each other. Do you remember? I have to admit to thinking—maybe it was the way you draped your sweaters around your shoulders and knotted them jauntily at your chest—that you were arrogant and self-absorbed. A bit priggish I'd have to say to be completely honest.

And then, last night. I was startled by your "Hello, Beth" as it broke through the muffled noises from the back porch and the harmony of insect sounds. In the dark your voice was deeper than I remembered from the library, the remnants of a midwest accent more pronounced.

Please excuse abrupt sign-off. Entire family has sudden urgent need to go online.

Date: Sunday, June 7, 9:29 P.M. EDT
From: SwimSlave
To: Wanderlust
Subj: Pardon Me?

What do you mean you thought of me in the past as harried, sort of a cross between hurried and worried?

Date: Sunday, June 7, 11:11 P.M. EDT
From: SwimSlave
To: Wanderlust
Subj: Okay, Truce

I agree, let's put past impressions behind us.

And I did want to say again, Thomas, how much I enjoyed last night, enjoyed standing with you at the intersection of our properties and talking the night away. Do you know that it was after midnight when I came inside to find the last of the guests gone and my husband, fully clothed, snoring loudly on my side of the bed? I tried to take the fact that he was on my side of the bed as a sign that he had missed me, that he'd tossed and turned, wondering where I was and what handsome stranger I might be talking to in the dark. Of course, in the morning Pete merely asked, "So what time did we go to bed, anyway?"

I'd like to say, too, that I am so very sorry that your wife has disappeared without a trace. It must have been awful to return from weeks and weeks away, which of course you need to do in your line of work, who can blame you there, and find someone you've been married to forever gone and not know where or for how long. And then to have your grown children refusing to speak to you on the phone. You seemed so sad, so needing to talk, and I'm happy you felt that you could talk to me.

And then your story about the rabbits . . . what was it you said? You had just liberated two domestic slaves from their inhumane captivity. Simply opened the door of their hutch, their prison, removed their figurative shackles, and allowed them the freedom nature had intended for them. Instinct will provide for them, you assured me, and I wondered if you were thinking about yourself, too.

It just occurred to me that I should have invited you to the cookout. How rude of me. You didn't wander over because you were *hungry*, did you? I'll remember to be more considerate in the future.

Good night.

Date:   Monday, June 8, 9:12 A.M. EDT
From:  SwimSlave
To:     Wanderlust
Subj:   Your Advice, Please

Do you have a minute, Thomas? The oddest thing has just happened in our yard. A couple of minutes ago, I stepped out of the shower and heard the sound of a motor idling in the driveway. I wiped a peephole in the steamy bathroom window and, sure enough, a Chem Lawn truck was just moving out of sight. Now, in and of itself, this would not be a big deal. Even though my idea of a beautiful yard is a shimmering field of wildflowers, years ago I deferred to my husband's need to pursue some astroturf vision of the perfect lawn. I try not to think about all the birds and chipmunks giving birth to genetically altered offspring.

The problem, Thomas, is that a similar vehicle from Green Grass Co. was here yesterday. My immediate and strong gut feeling today was that these two companies were not working cooperatively. Sure enough, when I changed quickly and ran outside to investigate, the evidence awaited me. A scattering of small green and black rectangles, stuck into the grass with matching metal picks, cried "Caution, recent chemical treatment, keep off grass!" The picks were lined up neatly beside nearly identical warnings in yellow and red that had been placed there yesterday.

I can't help but wonder, tangentially, is it possible that double spraying works like double negatives? If *I don't got no spray* means *I do have spray,* then does spraying twice mean that the wildflowers will win after all?

I would really like to blame this situation on someone other than myself. You see, I am absolutely certain I called only one lawn company, although I'm not quite as sure which of the two it was. And while Pete has been reminding me, rather naggingly I might add, to make that call for weeks and weeks, and I do remember him saying something about the need to hurry before grubs of some kind hatch, I don't remember him saying anything like never mind, Beth, I took care of it. Although I suppose there's always the chance that he said it when I wasn't listening.

The way I see it, I have several options. Confront him directly, forcefully, righteously. Because after all, this is not *my* fire to put out, and come to think of it, I'm sick of putting out all the family fires, whether they're mine or not.

Or I could just throw away those silly little rectangles, both color combinations. Or I could do nothing and just play dumb or I could discreetly pay both bills and cancel one of the lawn companies' future services.

So I guess that's actually three options.

Date:   Monday, June 8, 10:55 A.M. EDT
From:   SwimSlave
To:      Wanderlust
Subj:    How Sweet

You are simply too funny, Thomas.

I wandered out to the porch a few minutes ago, still contemplating the grass dilemma, and saw what you'd done. How adorable. I can't believe you managed to move all of the yellow and red signs from my yard to yours without my noticing.

I'm not sure you solved anything but you *did* make me laugh.

Date:  Tuesday, June 9, 7:59 A.M. EDT
From:  SwimSlave
To:    Wanderlust
Subj:  Bagels

I stopped to get bagels on the way home from swim practice this morning. I dropped off Margot and Chloe, who are fourteen and thirteen and finally both attending the same school again, then raced home to make sure P.J. would be ready in time to catch his bus. The whole time I was thinking how nice it would be to walk over to your house with some freshly brewed coffee and the rest of the bagels. Just to say hello and maybe have a quick chat before getting to work.

A couple of minutes ago I did just that. You did not appear to be home. The bagels are tucked inside your screen door. I hope you like sesame. I didn't leave the coffee, obviously.

Date: Tuesday, June 9, 9:35 A.M. EDT
From: SwimSlave
To: Wanderlust
Subj: Just Wondering

I was working away quite productively a few minutes ago, when it suddenly occurred to me that I wasn't sure if I had told you what I do for work. What I mean is that the whole time you were talking the other night about your adventures as a travel writer, I can't remember if I ever once jumped in and said, "Did you know I was a freelance quotation researcher, Thomas?" As Vanna White once said about her job on *Wheel of Fortune*: "It's not the most intellectual job in the world, but I do have to know the letters."

Still no sign of you. Good bagels last for only a day.

Date: Tuesday, June 9, 12:03 P.M. EDT
From: SwimSlave
To: Wanderlust
Subj: Oh. . . .

I simply can't believe you're gone, Thomas.

I almost dropped my sandwich, which I was carrying out to eat on the porch, when I saw the little bouquet of flowers you had left just inside the door. Were those from *my* garden? Did you know those tiny blue flowers are called forget-me-nots?

I found the note wrapped around the stems. And, Thomas, while I want you to know how very much I appreciate the flowers, and how very much I've enjoyed talking to you, I'm not 100 percent sure about your requests. Let me think about this.

Date: Tuesday, June 9, 12:13 P.M. EDT
From: SwimSlave
To: Wanderlust
Subj: Okay, I'm Back

I wish I knew how long you'll be gone, or even where you've gone. Your note said only that you'd be online as soon as possible. Actually you said *in*line but I knew that you were making a joke.

I think I can promise to let you know the instant I see any signs of Cindi, although I don't think I could possibly talk to her or get information from her. But, if your lawn service forgets to come and your lawn starts to look straggly, I will give a call to the number you left, I promise. The part about "given how adept you are at dealing with lawn companies", was that a joke?

And I really don't mind bringing in your mail for a bit. Our mailboxes share a pole so it's hardly an inconvenience.

Date: Wednesday, June 10, 8:05 P.M. EDT
From: SwimSlave

To: Wanderlust
Subj: Apology

Sorry to be so touchy yesterday, Thomas. I think I was just sad that you were gone. And while I hope you'll be back long before green mold could possibly overtake your front doorway, I want to assure you that I *did* remove the bagels.

I *will* keep an eye out for Cindi. I *will* guard against straggles in your lawn. I *will* collect your mail. I mean, what are friends for?

I was just sitting here looking at my beautiful bouquet of forget-me-nots. I thought of that quotation by Georgia O'Keeffe, the one about how nobody really sees a flower because it takes time, just like having a friend takes time. Or something like that. I'm sure I've got it in my files somewhere. Anyway, it made me think how much I *do* need a friend, Thomas.

Date: Thursday, June 11, 8:40 A.M. EDT
From: SwimSlave
To: Wanderlust
Subj: Rabbits

I'm hoping my notes are not becoming a nuisance. I'm especially wondering this since I have not heard a word from you yet. I'm picturing you somewhere exotic like Monaco or Kenya, in a walled resort or per-

20

haps a grass hut, basking in the incredible culture surrounding you. Maybe you can't find electricity for your computer, or a phone line, or whatever it is you need to plug in what I imagine to be the tiniest state-of-the art notebook.

I'm wondering why you never mentioned your destination. I'm wondering how often I should give you progress reports on your lawn, your mail, your wife. Nothing new to report in any of the three categories, although I suppose it *has* only been two days. Do you think Cindi is having her mail forwarded?

What I did notice, though, just as I was standing at the kitchen sink washing the breakfast dishes, was that your emancipated rabbits seem to have returned. First the larger grey one and then the smaller black-and-white rabbit jumped back into the hutch. The door *was* wide open but even so the jump must have been at least three to four feet (I'm guessing here and I admit to not being very good at judging heights).

I was surprised and curious enough to dry off my hands and tiptoe across the yard for a closer look. They didn't seem to be at all bothered by my presence, both just looked right at me with those soft bunny eyes. The larger one was calmly drinking from the water bottle, while the other one appeared, actually, to be using the litter box to relieve him or herself. Imagine, with all the outdoors at their disposal, or *for* their disposal!

I am wondering what I should do now. Should I change their water? I assume bacteria will begin to grow if it's left untended. And dirty litter boxes are absolute breeding grounds for disease. I remember reading that before we got our cat, Marilyn (who is now almost 17), and again when I was pregnant for the first time and wondering if it was safe to keep the cat or if it might somehow infect our as-yet-unborn child with some disease I can no longer remember the name of. I noticed, too, that just a small amount of pellet-shaped food remains in the bottom of that metal feeding contraption attached to the wire mesh at the front of the hutch. Should I refill it, and if so, what brand do they prefer?

Please advise.

Date:    Friday, June 12, 10:30 A.M. EDT
From:   SwimSlave
To:       Wanderlust
Subj:    Taking a Break

A most productive morning I've had, fueled by the knowledge that next week Margot, Chloe and P.J. will all finish school for the summer. Then it will be even harder to find pockets of uninterrupted time in which to work. Lately I seem to have fallen behind in my quotation quota. But this morning, instead of wondering where you are and if you've read my e-mail, I decided to get busy.

I even promised myself a treat. My solid morning effort would be rewarded with an afternoon of doing exactly what I want to do.

So as usual, I get up at 4:15 A.M., careful not to disturb Pete and P.J. as I gently but firmly wake the girls. In the kitchen I peel two bananas and slice five strawberries. I throw these and a large container of lowfat vanilla yogurt into the blender. I top the mixture with a splash of calcium-enriched orange juice. Covering the blender with a blanket to muffle the noise, I reach under and feel for the On switch. I leave the blender to its muffled whir just long enough to make sure all the lumps are gone. I feel around in a dark cabinet for three large insulated plastic cups. I fill two and, as always, pour whatever is left over into my cup. There are days when my cup is only a quarter full, others when I have to sip some off the top to avoid an overflow.

Margot and Chloe stumble through the kitchen, grabbing a drink with one hand and a swim bag, always packed the night before, with the other. Each of us slides into a pair of swim sandals from the vast collection lined up two by two, like animals waiting to board the ark, on the far wall of the mud room. I choose Speedo this morning, I think, but it could just as easily be TYR or Esprit or Adidas or Nike. We're in the car by 4:45. The girls fall asleep within minutes of drinking their breakfast, and I enjoy the dark, lonely roads more than you might imagine.

23

I pull up to the pool building just before 5:30, and the girls awaken when the motor starts to idle. They manage a mumbled, "Thanks, Mom," on the way out the door. I watch for a minute as they shuffle toward the pool entrance, thinking about how different they will look and sound when they emerge, chlorine-irritated red-white-and-blue eyes blinking, pool-soaked blonde hair several shades darker. They'll be crackling with energy and talking non-stop about this set and that time and who worked hard and who was a slacker.

Where was I going with all this? While I'm trying to remember, I'll send this much now. Is there a limit on how long e-mail can be? Wait—is the plural of e-mail, e-mail? Like deer is deer?

Date: Friday, June 12, 2:01 P.M. EDT
From: SwimSlave
To: Wanderlust
Subj: More

Maybe it's not important where I'm going with this, it's just nice to have someone to talk to. Well, so I don't leave any gaps, I'll start with the part where I drop Margot and Chloe at the pool. I head about a mile or so down the street to a far corner of the nearest beach parking lot. I change into white cotton socks and cross-trainers, and as I'm doing so, I happen to notice that I've only shaved one leg. Does that happen to men, Thomas, do they get so busy, maybe distracted is a better word, that they forget to finish shaving their faces? I don't think Pete ever does, but he sometimes does forget that he has tiny pieces of bloodsoaked toilet paper sticking to his cheeks.

I decide no one on the beach will notice my single nubby leg but I'll pay more attention to grooming in the future. Then I lock the car, hide the keys behind the front left tire and take a brisk walk on the beach. As I'm walking along, circumventing rocks and breathing in low tide, a quotation from Nietzsche pops into my head. It's the one where he says that when his creative energy flows the most freely, his muscular energy is the greatest and that he might often be seen dancing.

In twenty minutes I'm back at my car, feeling virtuous, if slightly tight through the calves. I pull my trusty purple milk crate from the trunk. Crammed into it are books of quotations, files I've made of quotations, blank index cards and a large assortment of pens and markers. I decide I'm in the mood for purple ink on a yellow card (unlined), and I write down what I remember of the Nietzsche quotation. I search for it in my files but can't find it under N. I look under P for philosopher but it's not there either. I decide to move on.

I do most of my work for a publishing company that makes "Quote-a-Day" journals. Right now they have me focusing on three priority areas: art and artist quotations, same-sex love quotations and quotes for left-handers. The good thing is that I don't often have to ponder the appropriate category for the sayings I find, although I suppose it's possible that I could run across something by a gay left-handed artist.

I find a quotation by Pascal that I really like. "The heart has its reasons which reason knows nothing of." I decide it's a perfect fit for the art and artist journal, even though Pascal was a scientist. Still, it works somehow, the connection between art and the heart. Just in case, though, you don't happen to know anything about Pascal's sex life or dominant side, do you, Thomas?

I find a gorgeous quotation by Jean Anouilh about how the object of art is to give shape to life and make it truer than true. Then I decide I have been sufficiently productive and that, after writing to you, I can do whatever I want for the rest of the day, until the kids get home and it's time to drive to the afternoon swim practice.

Will you look at the time?

Date:   Saturday, June 13, 8:00 A.M. EDT
From:   SwimSlave
To:     Wanderlust
Subj:   Guess What!

Thomas, you're not going to believe this but I finally have something to tell you about Cindi! Early this morn-

26

ing, Pete took the girls into Boston, which is where all the suburban satellites of their swim team converge for Saturday morning practice. P.J. was sleeping late, as he's been doing more and more often since turning ten, so I sat at the kitchen window contentedly sipping coffee, making a grocery list, patting Marilyn and looking out the window for the rabbits. (We have worked out a nice arrangement, the rabbits and I: they come and go as they please and I feed and water them and keep their litter box clean.)

Anyway, I finished the grocery list, left a note on the counter for P.J., and raced to the store so that I could be back in time to take P.J. shopping for a present on the way to a friend's birthday party. Instead of shopping at Shaw's on Rte. 3A as I usually do, I decided it would be quicker and easier, if more expensive, to go to the Fruit Center. I was standing near the cheese and dips, mesmerized for a moment by the incredible array of hummus, which I had no intention of even buying. I suddenly became aware of a conversation happening to my right, just past a display of boboli, which obscured my view of the speakers. I strained to listen to one woman telling another that Cindi, *your Cindi,* had called to make an appointment with a lawyer whom a friend of her friend worked for and the lawyer was— sorry about this, Thomas—a divorce lawyer.

You must be wondering how I knew they were talking about *your* Cindi. I admit that at first I wasn't sure. It could as easily have been some other Cindi they were talking about. Or I suppose even a *Cindy*. Suffice it to say that the spoken name alone was enough to arouse my suspicions. I peeked around the boboli stand to find out who the speakers were, and I must have been closer to them than I thought, because suddenly my face was right in theirs. They looked up, startled and not very friendly, and I'm afraid I turned all red and stammered an apology. I hate when I grovel like that. Anyway, the two women were Cindi's tennis friends. I'm sure of it because I've seen them in your driveway. So it must be *your* Cindi they were talking about. I mean, how many Cindis who play tennis could be contemplating divorce right now?

Maybe you should talk to a divorce lawyer, too, Thomas. Just to get some information, just in case. Not that I'm saying that I think you're going to get divorced. I mean, after all, everything could still work out, couldn't it? Of course, you'll have to *find* Cindi first to really know.

I hope the news about Cindi wasn't too much of a surprise. I hope I haven't made you sadder than you already are. I hope you will write to me soon.

Date: Saturday, June 13, 8:27 P.M. EDT
From: SwimSlave
To:     Wanderlust
Subj:  About Cindi

Did I overstep my bounds in this morning's e-mail? Did I say too much about Cindi? I think I'm going to wait until I hear from you to write again. I hope that doesn't hurt your feelings.

Date:   Monday, June 29, 2:03 P.M. EDT
From:  SwimSlave
To:     Wanderlust
Subj:  Yoo Hoo!

Oh, Thomas, come out, come out wherever you are! Your mail (mostly of the junk variety, it seems, although to my very quick glance it appears that there might be a few interesting items there) has gone from a small pile on the kitchen counter to a medium-sized wicker basket under the counter to a rather large two-handled shopping bag on the floor of the mud room. Pete tripped over it this morning on his way out the door to work. Fortunately the coffee he spilled missed his shirt and tie.

"What the hell is all this anyway?" he asked, gesturing to your bag of mail.

"Oh, just some mail I'm collecting for a friend."

On the way out the door Pete mumbled something like, "As if we don't have enough accumulated paper in this house already. . .".

"You have a nice day, too, honey," I said to his disappearing car. Wouldn't you think he would have asked, *what* friend?

It seems that I am not the only one who is waiting to hear from you. A man from your lawn service knocked this morning to ask if I knew how to get in touch with you. He said you are only paid up through the end of this month and, as it is their busy season, they simply won't be able to continue mowing for you unless they receive a check for July.

Since school ended for the summer, I have almost no time to myself for anything, so I hope it won't offend you if I don't write again until I hear from you. I have been not writing to you for over two weeks, but, in the interest of clear communication, I wanted to make sure you knew what I was *not* doing.

Date:   Sunday, July 5, 3:42 A.M. EDT
From:   SwimSlave
To:     Wanderlust
Subj:   About Last Night

Okay, I'm going to make an exception and write to you just one more time. Several hours ago I tried talking to Pete about how I'm feeling but he fell asleep in the middle of what I thought was a fairly compelling sentence.

So, Thomas, my hope is that maybe you can make me laugh by telling me an even worse reunion story. You

30

see, tonight, or I guess by now it is last night, was my twenty-fifth high school reunion, held on a brightly lit boat in the middle of Boston Harbor as fireworks exploded all over the city. And while the boat rocked with lots of great songs from the '70s: "Play That Funky Music" (I can't believe I forgot that was Wild Cherry) "Let's Get It On" and "We're an American Band", I had the saddest revelation of my life.

I guess I should back up a bit. The day started badly. I woke up early with an itchy right cheekbone. And even though I tried and tried not to scratch it, every five minutes or so when I looked in the mirror to see whether it was a pimple or hives or the start of a malignant melanoma, my right cheek was redder and more swollen. All I could imagine was going to my reunion and having everyone whisper, "Beth Riordan is here, did you see her? What is that *thing* on her cheek?"

By noon I decided I needed medical assistance. I headed for the mall's walk-in healthcare place because I figured if all went well, I'd have time to pick up some earrings to go with my new outfit on the way home. And I knew my regular doctor would never have office hours on the Fourth of July weekend.

I checked in with an unfriendly woman at a curved faux-granite reception desk. When I asked her what she thought of my cheek, she simply raised her eyebrows and told me to please take a seat. And then I waited. And waited.

Finally, over two hours and eight or ten magazines later, I followed a fast-walking doctor into an examining room barely large enough to hold two people. I sat on the examining table; he looked at my cheek. He scrawled something on a sheet of paper; I loped behind him as he led me back to the reception desk and handed my file to the receptionist.

"That'll be fifty-four dollars," said the receptionist as the doctor disappeared.

"But, what's wrong with me?" I asked.

The receptionist handed me the sheet of paper. The doctor had scrawled in surprisingly legible handwriting: "Patient's face unremarkable."

"That's it?" I asked. "That's it?" And then the receptionist, who wasn't such a bad sort after all, opened a cabinet and handed me three rectangular foil packets of sunscreen.

I forgot all about buying earrings and the whole way home I kept thinking, that damn doctor didn't even write, "Patient's *cheek* unremarkable." He said *face*.

Date:   Sunday, July 5, 6:21 A.M. EDT
From:   SwimSlave
To:     Wanderlust
Subj:   About Last Night, Cont'd

Sorry, Thomas. I just needed a few hours of sleep before
I could tell you the rest. Pete and I went to the reunion
with my friend, Heather, and her second husband,
Dave. You've probably seen Heather in my driveway
lots of times. You would have noticed her—men always
do. (She's the one with the great legs and wild outfits,
and her hair is usually red but occasionally some other
color.) Heather and I have been friends since elemen-
tary school. Sometimes I think she's my one true friend;
other times I think our friendship is just habit, so deeply
entrenched it's no longer a choice.

I had just finished telling Pete the story about my cheek
when Heather and Dave arrived. "I told you there was
nothing wrong with you," Pete said, one hand on the
doorknob.

"No, you didn't. You said you thought I should get it
looked at."

"Where did you get *that*?" Pete looked at me as if he
was not only irritated but genuinely puzzled. I wondered, as I have often lately, if one of us is starting to
speak another language. Then Pete opened the door

and we both made an effort to behave like a happy couple.

The reunion was fun at first. Dave, who I have to admit I like slightly better than Heather's first husband, hung out with us while Heather flirted her way around the room. Finally she came back, beaming about everyone telling her that she was the least changed. Pete and I slow-danced for a while to "Touch Me in the Morning" and "Killing Me Softly with His Song", and I tried to remember how long it had been since we'd had even that much romance in our lives. I think the romance goes first and then the sex, don't you, Thomas? At first I hardly noticed, the kids took up so much time, life was so busy. And then one day I realized sex had become one more thing we didn't have time for.

Still, we go through the motions sometimes. As we were dancing, Pete kissed me lightly on the neck and then whispered, "You look so beautiful tonight, Beth."

I tucked a piece of hair behind his ear and reached up to cover his eyes with my hands. "Okay, so what am I wearing?"

This is a sort of uneasy joke between us since a few months ago when Pete and I were getting ready for a party. He came into the kitchen to find me fully done up (hair, makeup and earrings) but still wearing my bathrobe. He looked at the same bathrobe he's been looking at for *years,* and actually asked, "Is that a new dress?"

Later he tried to tell me that it was the earrings that confused him, as if it was somehow my intention to trick him. But the truth is, he doesn't really look at me anymore.

Pete and I headed back to our table. A group was gathered around looking at a yearbook from junior high. Now I still have my high school yearbook, of course, but I didn't even remember that we had a yearbook in junior high. Someone said, "Look, Beth, you're on every page."

It wasn't much of a yearbook, just a shiny cardboard cover holding a couple of dozen pages but, you know something, Thomas, I *was* on practically every page. The pictures must have all been taken the same day because in each one I was wearing the same knee-length skirt and what I suddenly remembered was called a "poor boy" shirt, a simple scoop-necked knitted jersey with a pocket over one breast. I had hair that looked like Marlo Thomas's, shiny straight hair with a little flip at the ends, hair that I don't remember ever having. I had a Marlo Thomas smile, too, big and sincere and confident. I flipped through the pages, looking for that girl who looked like *That Girl.*

35

"Look, honey," I said, thinking Pete would be charmed.

Pete glanced over my shoulder for half a second, not even enough time to focus. "You're even more gorgeous now," he said, looking up at my former classmates with a grin that said, am I a great husband or what?

I went back to my yearbook. It was very much like looking through one of P.J.'s old *Where's Waldo* books. If I searched carefully, I could find a slightly different version of the same smiling girl in almost every picture—legs crossed or uncrossed, sitting at the end of a row of bleachers or in the middle, hands clasped in her lap or out-of-sight behind her back. How could it have been that I was a member of the chorus, the photography club, the honor society, the drama club *and* a cheerleader? I don't even remember holding the pompoms, let alone doing any splits.

And then it came to me, Thomas. I peaked in junior high. That was it. My high point. My pinnacle. My zenith. My apex. My climax. And I never even took the time to appreciate it, to say, wow, isn't it great to feel invincible, to have so many *choices*.

Did you ever feel that way, Thomas? That you could be anything and everything? Thanks for listening to all this. (Although I can only be sure you're listening *when you write back*.)

Date:   Thursday, July 9, 8:42 A.M. EDT
From:   SwimSlave
To:     Wanderlust
Subj:   Your Lawn

I'm writing to you again, Thomas, because I felt you should know that your lawn is a mess. Long and unkempt, just what I promised to look out for. I mentioned to Pete that we might pay your lawn service for just a week or two, knowing that we could trust you to pay us back, and he said absolutely not, we barely know you. I thought for a minute about contradicting that assumption and telling Pete that I have, in fact, been spending a fair amount of time corresponding with you, even if you have not been spending quite as much corresponding back. I tried to imagine him getting jealous but I couldn't see it.

We're leaving in a couple of hours for a weekend swim meet at the University of Connecticut. I hope the rabbits will be okay.

Date:   Monday, July 13, 12:33 P.M. EDT
From:   SwimSlave
To:     Wanderlust
Subj:   At Last!

Finally! It was wonderful to find your e-mail waiting for me when we got back late last night. (The rabbits were fine, in case you were worried.) I found myself holding my breath while the computer warmed up, and I admit that I became quite elated when I saw virtual mail in the virtual mailbox. It could have been from someone else, since I sometimes exchange e-mail(s) with my sisters, and sometimes Heather sends me off-color Internet jokes, but somehow I just *knew* it was from you.

Thanks for telling me that I still look like Marlo Thomas and reassuring me that no one ever has a good time at class reunions. But my favorite sentence of your beautiful e-mail was this: "Your energetic and delightful correspondence, Beth, breathes new life into this tired old soul."

Is it that bad, Thomas, the way you're feeling now? Does hearing from me really help? Do you really find my writing interesting? I wish I could say something truly original but I'm always afraid that everything worth saying may have already been said. It occurs to me that most people go through their whole lives without ever saying anything original, but the difference is that, unlike me, they don't *realize* they haven't said anything original. I guess that's an occupational hazard of quotation research.

It's like this, I'll want to say something about friendship and I'll think, Emerson, "A friend may well be reckoned the masterpiece of Nature." Then, right away, I'll think E.B. White, ". . . being with you is like walking on a very clear morning—definitely the sensation of belonging there." Next will come Walt Whitman, "Oh my friend, you have no way of knowing how longingly I look at you."

Or my mind will wander over to love and I'm assaulted by a jumble of quotes of *Love means never having to say you're sorry* and *Love is a many splendored thing* and *Love makes the world go round* and *Love, ageless* and however the rest of it goes.

It's exhausting. How can a person even think in the midst of this barrage? If I ever do come up with something unique to say about love or anything else, I'm sure I'll spend the rest of my life trying to make sure I'm not plagiarizing anyone. Mark Twain once said that Adam was the only man who, when he said something good, knew that nobody had said it before him. That quotation has always bothered me, though. I think Twain should have mentioned Eve, too, instead of excluding half the world's population.

How do you feel about *your* work, Thomas? Are you able to say things that are original in your writing, things that make a difference? In your e-mail you said you've almost finished your 14th travel book, *A Walking Tour of Laughlin, Nevada.* (Not Monaco, perhaps, but I *did* have the gambling part right, didn't I?) I'm sure it will be the best book ever written about Laughlin but is it what you want to be writing, Thomas? Do you find room there for creativity, for growth? For passion?

Just a few things I've been wondering about in my spare time. Your check for the lawn came in this morning's mail, as you promised. I'll take it directly to the lawn service so that they can mow right away. On the way there, I'll stop at the post office to forward your mail. I'll send the things that look important by Priority Mail, the rest I'll send Book Rate. Don't worry about reimbursing me for the postage.

Date: Monday, July 13, 9:10 P.M. EDT
From: SwimSlave
To: Wanderlust
Subj: P.S.

About your mail . . . the man in the post office said that Book Rate was only for printed matter, not for correspondence of any kind. When I explained to him that I wasn't actually *corresponding,* I was merely trying to *forward* correspondence, he looked at me as if I had come to the post office to buy a gallon of milk.

And then this nasty little man told me, rather disdainfully, that one doesn't have to pay to *forward* mail. He strutted back and forth a few times behind the counter and then informed me I'd have to fill out a forwarding address form for you. I stood there frozen, feeling the impatience of the people in the line behind me. Finally, I thought, I don't have to do anything I don't want to do. I didn't say that, of course, no sense adding rudeness to rudeness. But I just took the form, turned right around and walked to my car with everything—Priority Mail, illegal Book Rate mail and forwarding form.

I sat in the car thinking for awhile and then I drove to another post office a couple of miles away, where I just mailed everything Priority. What the hell, I figured. I ripped up the forwarding form and threw it in the trash. I mean, I don't know how long you'll actually be in Laughlin. And I don't really mind handling your mail. It's just one more way for us to stay connected.

I just reread the e-mail I sent earlier today and noticed it was neither particularly energetic nor original and so I thought that since I had a bit of free time this evening while the rest of the family is watching something silly on television, I'd try to entertain you with the weekend's excitement or lack thereof.

Remember last Thursday when I told you we were heading off to a weekend swim meet at the University of Connecticut? Well, right after I sent your e-mail that day, we loaded up the kids in the car and headed for Storrs, Connecticut. Did you ever notice my children, Thomas, as they toddled past you when your own two were just entering adolescence? Margot is the classic firstborn, driven to excel both in and out of the pool. Chloe is just a year behind and for a month each year in the fall they are both the same age. She swims, too, but only because, quite honestly, we make her. If left on her own, she would simply experiment with hairstyles and chase after boys.

P.J. is the baby at 10. He doesn't swim at all, probably because Pete and I ran out of energy to insist by the time he came along. He has a kind of quiet genius that satisfies Pete with its focus and intensity, and I suppose I love to watch his dreaminess. P.J. is a collector—currently it's anything to do with the military. He collects action soldiers and weaponry, creates complicated battle scenes, and then sketches them in his notebook. Sometimes he designs uniforms in drawings that have an amazing resemblance to high fashion design.

Now where was I? About to take you on a short trip with my family. Okay, on this particular morning, on this particularly beautiful day, everything that defines us as a family is moving along just like clockwork. Pete is driving too quickly and aggressively as always and by the time we get to the highway, we're doing our driving dance: I tell him he's going too fast and making me nervous and he tells me *I'm* making *him* nervous by *my* being nervous and he's not going any faster than anyone else on the road. Pete sees driving as a thing of moral significance. It doesn't matter if we all die in a high-speed, tragic accident; what matters is that He Is Right and that Other Drivers Are Wrong.

Sometimes I fantasize that if Pete and I divorce I'd never have to ride in a car with him again. And then I look over at him quickly, wondering if he can feel what I'm thinking. Or even if he's thinking what I'm thinking. That if we got divorced he wouldn't have to ride in a car with me again.

Then Pete invariably looks over at me and says, "So, we're making pretty good time, considering." Considering what? I want to say. Considering we're all still alive?

A few minutes onto the turnpike, Chloe, in a singsong voice, starts one of her favorite games: "If I married Matt Dillon, I'd be Chloe Dillon . . . if I married Ben Affleck, I'd be Chloe Affleck . . . if I married Leonardo diCaprio. . . ."

P.J. pulls himself away from his army reverie. "If you married David Bowie, you'd be Chlowie Bowie . . . if you married Vincent Van Gogh, you'd be Chloghie Van Goghie . . . if you married Curt Cobain, you'd be a necrophiliac!"

"Mom, make him stop!"

"Mom, tell them both to cut it out. I can't hear my music." Margot slides her headphones down to rest on her shoulders. A tinny version of the theme from *Rocky* raises the noise level even higher. Margot's big on the benefits of pre-competition motivational music.

"Beth, I can't drive with this racket!" Pete shouts, as if he were someone other than the father. This is when I want to cover my ears, close my eyes and shriek as loudly as I can. Why am I the one who is supposed to solve this stuff? When the kids look back on their childhood, Dad will be the fun guy and I will be mean old Mom who made them sit on their hands in silence the rest of the way to Connecticut.

Thanks for listening, especially since this letter wasn't quite as cheery as I had planned. I always feel so much better after I write to you. And I'd love to hear what *your* family did to drive *you* crazy.

Date:   Tuesday, July 14, 9:21 A.M. EDT
From:   SwimSlave
To:      Wanderlust
Subj:   Feeling Better

I woke up this morning thinking of course I can make my life sound more interesting, more original, more delightful than last night's effort. Pete and I might have run out of new things to say to each other, but the good news is that we don't fight with each other much either. Is that how it was between you and Cindi, and if so, how long did that stage last? I do wish you'd write to me and tell me if there are any new developments.

Have you heard from Cindi's lawyer? Have you maybe even heard from Cindi? How is your book going?

In the meantime, and I thought this through while I walked during swim practice this morning, I think I'll jump to the part in my weekend story when the driving, which really is the worst of it, is over. Entering the town of Storrs and seeing the signs for the University of Connecticut, it's hard to believe that UConn is much more than a big cow pasture. Lots of mooing and a definite scent of manure in the air. It's the kind of college I can imagine sending any of my three kids off to and feeling safe. I mean what could actually happen to them in a place that looks this clean? Later, when I ask the Reservations clerk at the hotel what the college kids do for fun, she twirls her hair around her finger and tells me that last night she went to a keg party in a cornfield and that was kinda fun. I revise my opinion immediately because even I can imagine that a lot can happen in a drunken cornfield.

We drive until we find the natatorium. It's overflowing with swimmers from all over New England. Hundreds of families whose kids have broad shoulders, narrow torsos and wet hair.

My daughters' team is big enough to take over the hotel we're staying in—a brand new Connecticut Courtyard that must be making a killing in the long distance truckers' market. Huge parking lots filled with only the trailers of 18-wheelers. After some contemplation, I realize the truckers must be driving around in the detached front cabs, a possibility I've never considered. They seem out of place in the shiny new hotel but they probably feel the same way about the swim families. Every single guest fits into either one of the two categories and the contrast is sharply apparent. (Please don't think that I am in any way judgmental of truck drivers, Thomas. In fact, this was my first and only time knowingly observing any and it could be that there are many varieties.)

We have a quick cheese pizza and salad with the kids plus fresh fruit and spring water and then Pete leaves to take Margot to the distance events, traditionally swum on the Thursday night of weekend meets. Margot loves the longer distances. She says she finds a rhythm and that it somehow makes more sense to keep swimming than it would to stop. Chloe hates long distances. She's a sprinter, fast in, fast out and back to whatever socializing she's momentarily interrupted.

Sorry, Thomas, duty calls—quite loudly, I might add, in the form of one hungry cat named Marilyn.

Date:  Wednesday, July 15, 9:43 A.M. EDT
From:  SwimSlave
To:    Wanderlust
Subj:  Continued

Did you miss me? So where was I? Right. The truckers. Pete and Margot leave for the meet, and Chloe, P.J. and I head down the hallway to the fancy new indoor pool at the hotel. Chloe finds some other swimmers to hang out with and P.J. starts to assemble a battle reenactment scene underneath the table where I am sitting. I notice scattered groupings of truckers at some of the tables. Several have placed six-packs of beer on top of the round poolside tables. I'd never really noticed before how the plastic rings left behind when a beer is removed make such convenient carrying handles. Neatly, as one trucker finishes a beer, he crunches it with a single bare hand, then arcs it high into the nearest trash basket. P.J. leans out from under the table far enough so that I can see the top of his brown curls and I know this can-crushing behavior is something that we'll start seeing at home.

I open my own serving of seltzer and flip through a magazine. Time plods along as it always does on the first evening of a swim weekend, before we settle into the routine. I begin reading an article entitled "101 Ways to Spice Up Your Life", which turns out to be only about *cooking*. Disappointed, I skim for something more interesting until my mother's radar picks up a disturbance in the area. I peek under the table to check P.J. first but he is merely giving orders to squadrons of plastic men.

I turn to the nearest trucker table and they are definitely leering with that kind of male energy you feel walking by a construction site on a hot summer's day in a sundress. The occupants of the next closest table are alert, too, and I don't like the looks on their faces. Quickly I follow their gaze across the pool area.

Chloe and her friends, three 13-year-olds in bikinis, are parading back and forth at the far end of the pool in a kind of adolescent, hormone-fueled version of a beauty pageant. They bear an unmistakable—if cleaner cut—resemblance to teenage prostitutes. And now, one by one, with wiggling hips and flirtatious shakes of the head, they stroll along an imaginary runway (for lack of a diving board) and execute a flamboyant entry into the water with one hand on hip, the other behind the head. The other girls applaud with what I'm sure they imagine is sophistication and when their friend breaks the surface they actually hold fingers up to score her performance.

Oh my God. The truckers are starting to join in with quiet applause and one extends ten fingers furtively. I lean down to P.J. and tell him through clenched teeth to pack up quickly. I remind myself that I am a grownup, slide my chair back and begin to walk across the pool area. I am extremely conscious of not moving my hips and, as a result, I may have begun to waddle slightly. Children and truckers watch my every move. My mind jumps suddenly to a much-publicized gang rape in Rhode Island last year. I wonder if this is how the air felt just before it happened: the sudden quiet, the holding of breath all around, the frightening sexual energy, the belated regret for introducing a game that wasn't a game anymore.

"Chloe, get your things and come with me right now," I say quietly. It is a given that the other girls will follow. Chloe is the clear leader; I am the adult with temporary authority. Single file, in the still silent room, we begin to walk. I am holding my head high and my vision is completely focused on a point across the room, slightly above and beyond the table where P.J. is waiting. Unbelievably, when we get there, one of the truckers is sitting on the floor with him, one of P.J.'s soldiers in his hand.

"Mom, can I stay here and play with Bud?" P.J. asks. The Bud person looks at me and I avoid his eyes.

"No, honey, it's time for us all to leave," I answer, fighting to keep the shaking out of my voice, my hands. And we do leave, and, of course, when we're almost to the door a nasty, quiet laughter begins along with a falsetto replay of my parting words. I feel my cheeks burning and when we're long out of sight I tell the girls, who are amazingly unconcerned, what a scary thing they have done. They listen to me with feigned respect and nod their heads in a way that makes me want to kill them.

When Pete gets back to the hotel with Margot, I tell him the whole story. He picks up Margot's swim book and starts recording her latest times. When he finally glances up, he says, "Beth, what's your point? What are you telling me actually happened? The kids were playing and the truckers were watching them instead of you? Is that it?"

Date: Thursday, July 16, 10:30 A.M. EDT
From: SwimSlave
To: Wanderlust
Subj: I Give Up

I just couldn't finish the swim weekend story. I'm still in shock over Pete's trucker comment. Could he really miss the point so completely or was he just trying to pick a fight? Did I really want those unappealing guys to look at me instead of the girls? Oh no, before long I'll be one of those middle-aged women who wear miniskirts and false eyelashes, like Chloe's classmate's mother who, rumor has it, wore her eight-year-old daughter's ballet tutu to a Halloween party.

We leave this afternoon for a weekend at Brown University. Then next weekend we'll stay in Cambridge for the New England Championships at Harvard. AND THEN THE SEASON WILL BE OVER!! We will all have three entire weeks without swimming and quite possibly without seeing a single trucker. Hard to imagine what to do with all that free time. Heather wants me to go with her for a week to one of those adult "ropes course" challenge programs. She says it's much more than scaling walls and swinging from tree to tree. It is, according to Heather, about challenging yourself as a person, team building with other adults, and finding out who you really are and what you really want. I told Heather I'm not sure I even want to know all that. What's the point? What if I go to all that trouble figuring out who I really am and what I really want and then I can't have it?

Heather is always experimenting, always trying something new, yet I don't see her figuring out much more than the rest of us. Her last Big Adventure involved goats. Somehow she decided that she and her family needed more joy in their lives and that goats were the animals that bring the most joy. Now where do you even *get* that idea? I mean are there people who go around measuring how much joy-bringing potential various animals have? Dogs are a nine and cats a seven and ferrets a six and that sort of thing? I remember Heather couldn't answer those questions but she got the goats anyway. Actually it was one mother goat but she was pregnant with twins.

And right from the start, it seemed not all that joyful from my perspective. First of all, Heather was told by the person who sold her the pregnant goat that the gestation period for goat pregnancies was exactly four months. So her family planned their summer vacation for the start of the fifth month figuring that by then the kids and their mother would be old enough to be fed by a neighbor. But it turns out that a goat's pregnancy lasts exactly five months, *not* four months, so they had to give up the deposit they'd put on a house on Cape Cod for that week. Dave thought they should return the goat to the person who'd sold it to them under false-length-of-pregnancy pretenses. Heather felt that the opportunity for the family to witness the miracle of goat birth far outweighed the forfeited deposit.

Heather won out and the entire family attended the birth. Twins are never easy, especially for goats it seems. The mother thrashed and bleated and Heather's younger daughter ran to her room and hid under her bed. The older daughter stayed, yelling, "gross!" and "disgusting!" and "I'm never doing that!"

Two days later the mother goat had a raging breast infection. She needed to be milked every hour round the clock and Heather was the only one she would let near her. Then, because the mother didn't want the kids anywhere near her, they had to be fed by bottle with the expressed milk, which took most of the rest of the hour. By then, Heather was having vivid flashbacks, brought on by severe sleep deprivation, to the breast infections of her own nursing days.

A lot of work for very little joy, if you ask me. But Heather regroups quickly, and when I stopped by with my human kids last week, she was happily clipping goat

cheese recipes and inviting me to go to the adult challenge program with her.

Have you ever gone on a trip like this, Thomas, or better yet, written a how-to manual? Do you think I should
go? Do you think I only want to go to get a break from
Pete, and, if so, is that a good enough reason?

I'll write when we get back from Brown.

Date:  Monday, July 20, 8:32 A.M. EDT
From:  SwimSlave
To:    Wanderlust
Subj:  Struggling to Stay Awake

4:15 came early this morning, let me tell you. You'd
think if the coaches didn't want to give the swimmers
a morning off after a grueling weekend, they'd do it for
the sake of the parents. Sometimes I think that it would
be easier to just enlist the whole family in the Marines.

There's a little downtown strip a short walk from the
Brown campus. Good food but an iffy feeling as if the
area is either on its way up or down. The local bikers
pull their motorcycles up to the curb and then turn
them around, facing out into the street at an angle.
They shut off the engines and just sit there checking out
the college girls. I imagine that if one of them sees the
girl he is looking for, he will swoop down on her like a

leather-clad Zeus, throw her onto the back of the bike before she can save herself, and she'll be lost forever. I decide that my children should not attend Brown. As I am enjoying a slice of pizzette with smoked mozzarella and fresh basil at an outdoor cafe, I'm sure I see drugs and money being exchanged on the upper deck of an apartment across the street. I look away before anyone notices me noticing them. One of the bikers dismounts long enough to enter a take-out restaurant and emerge with a bucket of ribs. When one of his neighbors asks him to share, he tells him to get his own fucking ribs.

I have a sudden urge to walk by these completely unappetizing bikers, from a safe distance of course, just to see if they'd turn their heads to look at me. Not that men ever quite drooled over me like they still do over Heather but they looked a lot. Not long ago when I was with my daughters, a man standing outside an office building appeared to be watching us as we walked down the street. When we got within earshot I wanted to stop and say, excuse me, sir, but how many of us are you looking at?

The minute we got home last night I turned on the computer to check my e-mail. A quick note from my sister in Chicago, an e-mail brochure of sorts forwarded to me by Heather—pictures of people in helmets dangling from a rock-climbing wall. I was so sad not to find even the tiniest note from you. . . .

Date: Tuesday, July 21, 8:52 A.M. EDT
From: SwimSlave
To: Wanderlust
Subj: The Beach

The beach was spectacular this morning. One thing about being all dressed, although not exactly dressed up, with nowhere to go at 5:30 in the morning is that there is nothing to do but get some exercise. Even the coffee shops don't open for another half hour.

I suppose I could hang around and chat with the other Swim Moms. But I've heard it all before. Suzie did a 28:79 in the 50 meter-free at Brown, which is just better than the senior cut of 29:39, but how could she have expected the junior national time when she's not even tapered yet. . . . That's really most of what they talk about, and the truth is that most of them, no matter how unrealistic it is, think that their child is going to be the ONE TO MAKE IT, to go all the way, to beat the odds and swim at Stanford and then the Olympics. I guess that's what keeps you going. The kids seem much more stable.

Sometimes the women start to talk about their husbands, their marriages. I wonder, is there a husband and wife out there who has been married for a couple of decades who still like each other? I'm not talking *love* here, I'm talking *like*. Pete and I don't even like the same food these days. He always wants to eat at a "chain" because he says he knows what he's getting, and I want to take a chance on some new restaurant just because it looks interesting.

Mostly I walk alone. This morning, as I started to say, was gorgeous. The tide was just beginning to roll back in and the beach was scattered with dozens and dozens of sand dollars, more than I've ever seen before. As I walked, I started collecting them in my hands, imagining what it might be like to just keep walking. I'd leave my car in the beach parking lot like those women you read about in the newspaper who simply disappear. I'd walk and walk until I found a new life I wanted to live. Maybe I'd just keep walking until I ended up in Laughlin, Nevada.

I brought the sand dollars home with me, where it suddenly occurred to me that I'm not sure how to tell if sand dollars are dead. If you have any information on that subject, I'd appreciate hearing it quickly because I have placed them evenly around the lip of our screened-in porch floor, the part outside of the house. I think the sun will bleach them white, and maybe even bleach the wood around them. Conceivably, if I wait a couple of weeks and then lift them up, their outline will show on the wood of the floorboards. Kind of a delicate, reverse stenciling, a reminder of all the times I've walked the beach and circled back toward home.

Date:   Wednesday, July 22, 11:37 A.M. EDT
From:   SwimSlave
To:     Wanderlust
Subj:   Trying to Work

Lately I find myself writing to you when I should be working. I hope that makes you feel a responsibility for writing back. As long as you want to, of course.

I really need to work. The ritual kind of pulls me in, and the momentum takes over. I love to flag quotations with hot pink and teal and purple Post-it®s. I am soothed by the sight of my handwriting as I copy the quotations onto 4 × 6 index cards, and delight in my efficiency as I type the quotations into documents on the computer. I've even thought to keep a file marked "miscellaneous," for quotations for future use. I guess my work is like a Japanese garden. Looked at without imagination, it's just a bunch of rocks and sand. But there is the joy of order there, of being allowed to rearrange the never-ending possibilities.

I was just getting into the flow this morning when Heather showed up unexpectedly, which is always the way Heather arrives. She was all excited because she just found an even better adult challenge program. It's called "Special Delivery" and it's just for women to learn to appreciate themselves through nature. Heather said there is usually a long waiting list but when she

57

called, two women had just canceled for the third week in August. Rather than take the chance of losing the spots, Heather just booked us. Heather said to trust her, that it would be a life-changing experience.

Would you have minded if Cindi had gone away for a wilderness self-discovery week, Thomas? I suppose it would have been better than what she did which was to just go away. Pete will not be thrilled. I think I'll downplay the expense and pay for it with my quotation money, which means I must get back to work.

Pete also will not like the fact that I'm going with Heather. He is always highly critical of what he calls her "phases". I have noticed, though, that when she's in the room, he is very attentive. I used to think he had a crush on her. Then for a while I thought he wanted her to like him even though he disapproved of her. Now I don't know what I think, except that when I mention the trip, I know he won't be happy.

It would be a nice surprise to have a message waiting when I get back from Cambridge.

Date:   Thursday, July 23, 2:03 P.M. EDT
From:   SwimSlave
To:      Wanderlust
Subj:    Alert!

Thomas, you are not going to believe this. We were just in the car, the whole family, in the driveway, ready to leave for Cambridge. I glanced at your house and CINDI'S VOLVO WAGON IS IN YOUR DRIVEWAY. RIGHT NOW.

I sneaked back into the house on the pretense of needing to use the bathroom but really to send you this message.

Date:   Sunday, July 26, 11:56 P.M. EDT
From:  SwimSlave
To:      Wanderlust
Subj:   Just Got Back

I tiptoed over to your house just now. No lights. No signs of Cindi. Please advise.

Date:   Monday, July 27, 9:11 A.M. EDT
From:  SwimSlave
To:      Wanderlust
Subj:   Sorry

I'm afraid I missed an opportunity this weekend, Thomas. Although I'm not quite sure what I could have done if I had been here. Cindi and I have never been exactly chatty. Still, I woke up this morning with the feeling that I had let you down.

The rabbits are well, if that's any consolation. Oh, and guess what I forgot to tell you? I know their names now.

One night last week, after dinner, P.J. picked up the leftover salad and said, "I think I'll take this out to Rainbow and Star." Just like that.

I was so startled I may have overreacted. "How did you find out their names?" I asked.

"Mom, those have *always* been their names," he answered. Then he added, "How could anybody just leave their rabbits like that?"

"Maybe they thought the rabbits would enjoy their freedom, honey," I ventured.

P.J., looking alarmingly like his father, gave me his first pure glance of cold, cruel, adolescent judgment. I felt as if I should run and find his baby book so that I could flip through the pages, past milestones like *First Step* and *First Time Said "Mommy"*, until I found the blank pages at the end of the book. There I would record *First Bad Attitude* with today's date.

Well, at least now I know that Rainbow is the bigger grey-colored bossy bunny and Star is the smaller black-and-white one with the cute little ears.

Date:   Tuesday, July 28, 8:49 A.M. EDT
From:   SwimSlave
To:      Wanderlust
Subj:   Hiatus

I awoke at 4:15 this morning as if I had a place to go. I rolled away from Pete's snoring and out of bed. I thought about Virginia Woolf saying that a woman must have a room of her own to write fiction. I decided that what Virginia Woolf really meant was that a woman needs a room of her own—period. I imagined moving into my own room and immediately the rest of my family following me there to see what I was doing.

Brief fantasy over, I walked quietly to the kitchen and made a cup of coffee to drink outside while I attempted to watch the sun rise between the breaks in the pine trees. The mosquitoes were as vicious as the view was impaired. I tiptoed back into bed just in time to pretend to be asleep when Pete's alarm went off at 6:00.

I stayed in bed, my heart racing from the caffeine, until I heard his car pull away at 6:45. I wondered if he would wake up and smell the coffee and ask me about it when he got home from work, and if he did, what I would say. And, most of all, I wondered why I was sneaking around like a trespasser in my own home. Was this some vague attempt to find my own room? If I kept moving out of everyone's path, would I actually find a place just for me?

Maybe I'm just exhausted from the championship swim weekend. Margot had top-eight finishes in just about everything, and managed to swim two top-sixteen national reportable times. That's a very big deal, Thomas, in case you don't know. Chloe spent most of the four days leading cheers and talking to friends. At the end of every meet, Pete always says something like this to her, "And it looks like you were unanimously voted Miss Congeniality again, Chlo. Did you get a trophy or just the set of luggage?" But Chloe found her focus right before the 50-freestyle and came in third. She has such incredible potential as a swimmer, cares so little about it, and seems so genuinely happy. There may or may not be a lesson in that.

In between sessions on Friday we hurried back to the hotel so that the girls could rest, Pete could make some business calls, and P.J. could have some hang-out time. As much as he balks at organized swimming, the pool is usually the first place he heads when he has a choice. We were in luck this afternoon and the hotel pool was empty. P.J. unpacked one of the bags and began to lay out an assortment of items. Apparently today would not be an army day.

I opened up a paperback copy of *Wuthering Heights,* which has been on my "to read" list for years. I have a hard time reading these days without skimming for quotations, and this poolside attempt proved to be no exception. I placed the book face down in my lap and watched as P.J. picked up one squirt gun with each hand, walked over to his tape player and pressed what

I assumed was the "Play" button. He turned and leaped into the water, then pulled himself up through a blown-up tube to a reclining position. He froze quickly for just a moment before the music began. Little Richard's "Tutti Frutti" blasted out of the little tapedeck and P.J. launched into a truly amazing performance. Staying with the beat of the song, he sculled first clockwise, then counterclockwise, executed a backwards somersault off the tube and reemerged through the hole, spraying water from his mouth. And every time Little Richard got to the *wop bop a loo bop a lop bam boom* part, P.J.'s squirt guns accompanied him with streams of water in all directions.

Not once did he look in my direction, not once did he need me to ooh and aah. This, whatever it was, was all for him. Finally, he came over to sit in the lounge chair next to mine. "P.J., that was great," I said.

"Thanks, Mom. Can we go eat?"

Date:   Wednesday, July 29, 5:01 A.M. EDT
From:   SwimSlave
To:     Wanderlust
Subj:   Productivity

I am not going to write to you today. I am going to grind out pages and pages of incredibly meaningful and, because I get paid by the word, incredibly long quotations for all three journals.

Date: Wednesday, July 29, 12:02 P.M. EDT
From: SwimSlave
To: Wanderlust
Subj: Yes!

It worked! Instead of writing to you, I thought about *you* writing to me, tried to think it hard enough that you would *feel* it. Thank you very much for your e-mail. By the way, what is the time difference between Nevada and Massachusetts? I like to think about what time of day it is for you when you write to me.

Do you really think that "motorcyclists and Zeus, as well as lesser gods, will be checking [me] out for years to come"? Such a sweet thing to say, Thomas.

Thanks for sharing so many details about your work. Writing travel books sounds fascinating, and what hard work, all those details to unearth. And Laughlin sounds like a real gem of a city.

Date: Wednesday, July 29, 2:14 P.M. EDT
From: SwimSlave
To: Wanderlust
Subj: P.S.

You didn't comment on the trip Heather is planning to drag me along on. What do you think?

Date: Friday, July 31, 5:22 A.M. EDT
From: SwimSlave

To:      Wanderlust
Subj:    Cranking Along

I telepathed e-mail requests to you all day yesterday but it doesn't seem to have worked yet. My kids are all sleeping till almost noon these days, leaving me the biggest chunk of work time for quotation excavation. . . . No problem finding same-sex love quotations. I mean what famous person isn't *at least* bisexual these days? The art/artist stuff is really easy to find, too. I just ran across that quotation by Renoir about how he has a "predilection for painting that lends joyousness to a wall". What if art is as simple as that? Just bringing joy.

I'm having a much more difficult time with the quotations for left-handers. I wonder if I can use anything said by anyone who is/was left-handed or do I have to find compelling quotations about *being* left-handed. I might just try submitting things like, "He who wishes to secure the good of others, has already secured his own."—Confucius, famous left-hander. Actually, I have no idea if Confucius was left-handed (do you?) but it's an idea.

To work. To work. To work.

Date:    Saturday, August 1, 11:37 A.M. EDT
From:    SwimSlave
To:      Wanderlust
Subj:    About Your Lawn

Someone from your lawn service came to our door a few minutes ago. I was upstairs so Pete answered. I came into the kitchen just in time to hear Pete telling him that we didn't have anything to do with you or your lawn.

I just stood there, not saying a word. I was trying to remember exactly when in my marriage it got easier to just say nothing.

But I peeked out the window and memorized the phone number on the lawn guy's truck. I'll call them later and tell them not to take you off their client list. Please send me the check as soon as possible. Also, there is another large pile of mail here. I moved it out of the kitchen and put it next to a pile of books near my desk. Where do you want me to send it?

Date: Saturday, August 1, 3:10 P.M. EDT
From: SwimSlave
To: Wanderlust
Subj: More About Your Lawn

Your lawn service wants a check IMMEDIATELY or they will give your slot to another customer. I almost offered to write a check on the spot and drive it right over to them but I could just hear Pete saying, "What are you, *crazy*?" if he found out.

Date: Saturday, August 1, 7:22 P.M. EDT
From: SwimSlave

To: Wanderlust
Subj: Even More About Your Lawn

Maybe I *should* have written that check. I hate to think that I'm the kind of person who just says, well, it's not *my* problem.

Date: Tuesday, August 4, 1:04 P.M. EDT
From: SwimSlave
To: Wanderlust
Subj: Oh, Thomas!

Your first real gift to me! And just when I was starting to doubt you, Thomas. I wouldn't be exaggerating if I said that the book that just this minute came in the mail is the nicest thing I've received from anyone in a long time. And how thoughtful to choose something that will help me with my research—*Southpaw Sages*—a whole book of quotations from left-handers. I haven't had a chance to look through it yet because first I wanted to run right to the computer and send you a thank-you note. I noticed the bookmark tucked inside said "Books for a Buck". I thought that was a New England chain of stores. Are you still in Laughlin? It just occurred to me that I don't really know where you are.

Just flew downstairs for a quick minute to look at the return address on the package. You *are* still in Laughlin. Which reminds me that I've been extremely rude in not asking how your book is coming along. I do care about it and anything else that matters to you, Thomas, so if you're planning to write to me soon, and I really hope that you are, please tell me everything and know in advance that I will be interested.

In the meantime, I will bring the check you enclosed to your lawn service within the hour. And of course I'll hold onto your mail UNTIL YOU GET HERE!!! I can't believe it's true, that you're going to be here before the end of the month. Promise me, though, that you will either come right away or that you'll wait until after the 23rd, which is the day I return from my trip with Heather. I would never have let her talk me into going if I had ever thought it would interfere with your visit. I leave on the 17th, so please cross those seven days off of your list of potential visiting days.

What am I talking about—visit? It is your home after all. Could it be that you're coming back to live for a while? Have you been in touch with Cindi? You always leave me wanting to know so much. . . .

Date: Wednesday, August 5, 5:50 A.M. EDT
From: SwimSlave
To: Wanderlust
Subj: Small Solitude

The best part of the day is just about over. I love the quiet morning sounds, the feeling of being completely alone to do anything I might feel like doing. Within minutes, I'll hear Pete's feet outside the door, and see his tousled and greying blond head peeking around the corner to ask what I'm doing. And I will not say, "What the hell does it look like I'm doing?" Maybe I'll tiptoe back to bed before the alarm goes off.

Bye for now.

Date:  Wednesday, August 5, 1:20 P.M. EDT
From:  SwimSlave
To:    Wanderlust
Subj:  Later

I was working away, in large part thanks to the nicest book that someone just gave me, and I could hear the radio one of the kids was playing downstairs, and I could just barely make out that old Fleetwood Mac song that has been re-released in a version that I think is better than the old. Anyway, I found myself trying to listen more closely and the words were something about don't stop thinking about tomorrow because it will soon be here.

Pete and I are taking the kids and their friends to Riverview Park tomorrow. Just overnight, but please don't come while we're gone. (Although if you do, could you check on the rabbits?)

Date:  Saturday, August 8, 5:31 A.M. EDT
From:  SwimSlave
To:    Wanderlust
Subj:  Back Again

I am absolutely exhausted but woke up early anyway to have some time alone. I always forget how much I hate water parks until I find myself in one again. Ugh. There are an amazing number of people wearing unflattering bathing suits, and it occurs to me that this would be a good place for *Glamour* or *Vogue* to shoot a "fashion don'ts" layout.

Hundreds of fleshy bodies are baking in the shadeless glare of a merciless sun, and I find myself holding in my uncooperative stomach, thinking I hope I don't look like *that*. Or *that*. There are endless lines of nasty parents screaming at their soon-to-be-as-nasty children. I am applauding myself for my superior parenting skills when Chloe interrupts to say, "Mom, I locked my key in my locker. What should *we* do?" I yell at her like the worst of them, and then have to wait in another long line with her, as she pouts, to have the locker opened by an attendant.

Eventually I find myself sitting alone with *Southpaw Sages* at a small white plastic table piled high with everyone's belongings. Did you know that Oprah Winfrey is a left-hander, and so were Marilyn Monroe and Joan of Arc?

When we arrive at the hotel that night, the Reservations kid (whatever happened to hiring adults?) hands us keys to rooms 832 and 833. All eight of us, our three children each towing a friend, cram into the elevator. When we get to our rooms, we find out that they do not have a connecting door. I call down to the youngster at the Reservations desk, who doesn't think it's all that big a problem, and suggests that we just rent two movies and tell everyone not to leave their rooms until morning. "Thank you so much for the parenting advice," I tell him. "But I'd rather you find us two adjoining rooms." Of course, all the porters are unavailable, probably off somewhere shaving for the first time. So we drag our stuff back to the elevator and by the time we reach Rooms 515 and 516 even the kids are ready to sleep.

The next morning we apply sunscreen in the parking lot outside the park, passing the SPF 15 stuff between the boys and Pete and me, while the girls giggle and cover themselves with some new glitter formula that turns them purple with shiny flecks of silver. We head inside and dump our things at the same table we had the day before. This does not feel like a particularly good thing, but like we might be stuck in water park limbo forever. Pete ignores me by reading the paper. I try on the idea that maybe Peter and I are simply saving up things to say when the kids move out. When P.J. heads off for college, perhaps we'll finally fall into each other's arms, as if there had been no lapse at all, and then talk the night away like we did before we didn't anymore.

Right around three o'clock the sky opens up with no warning and truckloads of rain pour down on us. Rookie parents grab their kids and make a run for their cars. Veteran parents know better. There is an unwritten but absolute rule that if you leave a water park before the day is over, your children will ask for a make-up trip. Pete looks for a dry place to use his cell phone to check with the office. I walk around in water swirling up to my ankles, stopping every few minutes to peel a candy wrapper or cigarette butt from one of my feet. I think of leeches in rice paddies.

Someone starts a rumor that the toilets have backed up into the wave pool. All six kids show up together, screaming about being contaminated. And yes, they are begging to leave.

You must remember taking trips like these, Thomas. What tricks did you and Cindi learn to avoid the clever traps your children set?

Date:  Sunday, August 9, 4:31 P.M. EDT
From:  SwimSlave
To:     Wanderlust
Subj:   Family Work Day

The entire family has spent the day working. Cutting back perennials that have gone by, bagging the refuse. Sorting through clothing, packing up the outgrown and no-longer-stylish. Loading up the returnable bottles and cans as well as the recyclable newspaper, plastic and aluminum that have been accumulating in the garage. All to be composted, recycled, donated or disposed of at the sanitary landfill, better known as "the dump". Heather corrects me when I say *dump*, yet she calls the pediatrician's office the *vet's*.

While we are working, Pete makes about a dozen inferences that we better get this done today since Your Mother will be deserting us soon. Now that I know for sure that he doesn't want me to go on this trip, I want to go after all.

Date:   Monday, August 10, 1:21 P.M. EDT
From:  SwimSlave
To:      Wanderlust
Subj:  Crazy Friend

I've changed my mind. Heather just left. This trip cannot possibly be a good thing. Heather drives a late model Mercedes, cream-colored with a very cushy brown leather interior. Anyway, have you ever met a Mercedes owner who puts bumper stickers on her car? Heather does. As a nod to understatement, she puts on only one at a time, which she changes once the shock value wears off. The last one was, "Bad cop, no donut". What an inflammatory statement to put on a car, especially when you drive the way Heather does. I was terrified to ride with her, thinking that we'd get pulled over by a cop who reads.

But that was nothing. Today Heather actually brought me outside to see her latest bumper sticker. It said, "Sorry I haven't been to church but I've been busy

practicing witchcraft and learning how to be a lesbian."
Now I know Heather is not a lesbian, at least I don't
know how she would have time for that with all the
men she says she either has, has just had, or is about to
have in her life. And I hope that this doesn't sound like
I have anything but the utmost respect for lesbians, but
I don't really want to go anywhere with Heather ever
again unless I drive my car.

Maybe I do want to go on the trip. Just not in Heather's
car.

Date:   Tuesday, August 11, 7:15 A.M. EDT
From:   SwimSlave
To:      Wanderlust
Subj:   Sleeping In

I managed to stay in bed until 6:00 and then had coffee and muffins with Pete this morning. I thought that
maybe if I made an effort, we could get back on more
pleasant footing. He just kept rattling off all the things
I should get done this week, before I leave on my trip.
Take the kids back-to-school shopping, pick the basil in
the garden before it goes to seed. . . . As if I ever needed
his prodding to get these things done before. As if he
ever even noticed if they got done.

Did Cindi ever nag you like this before you left on a trip?
It will be a good idea. For me to go, that is. Not for anyone to nag. Maybe after some time apart, we might be
able to enjoy each other's company again. When Pete

asks me how my day was, I won't feel the need to snap, "What do you mean by *that*?" I'm trying to imagine what it will feel like to miss my husband.

Date:   Tuesday, August 11, 1:05 P.M. EDT
From:   SwimSlave
To:     Wanderlust
Subj:   Another Gift!

I just checked my mail and found the gift you sent me. Thank you so much for the video of *Deliverance*. How nice of you, Thomas. I recognize the title. Is there a particular reason you chose that movie? Does it have something to do with the fact that the name of the trip I'm taking is "Special Delivery"?

Since you didn't enclose a note or letter, I guess I'll put the movie on now.

Date:   Tuesday, August 11, 4:30 P.M. EDT
From:   SwimSlave
To:     Wanderlust
Subj:   Thomas!

What a terrifying movie! You don't think my trip is going to be like that, do you? Canoes crashing down waterfalls, crazed backwoodsmen threatening to make the city folks squeal like pigs. . . . As I was watching the movie, I remembered seeing part of it on TV one night years ago. Pete tried to talk me into staying but I went upstairs to watch *Same Time, Next Year.* Watching

*Deliverance* again, I remembered one of the lines even before Burt Reynolds said it—"Sometimes you've got to lose yourself to find yourself."

You *were* being funny, weren't you?

Date:   Wednesday, August 12, 2:15 P.M. EDT
From:   SwimSlave
To:     Wanderlust
Subj:   Another Heather Visit

Heather came by this morning to consult on my wardrobe for the trip. Like I need one. I mean, after all, this is a wilderness trip. A finding-yourself, not finding-an-outfit, kind of trip. I said all of this and more to Heather but of course it didn't help much. Heather was talking khaki. Heather was talking hiking boots. Heather was talking getting her eyelashes dyed and her legs waxed so she'd "hold up" for the week. I pointed out that this was an all women's trip, not a singles soiree. "But surely you've read my latest bumper sticker . . ." Heather said with a rather menacing wiggle of her eyebrows.

"Heather's gay! Heather's gay!" taunted P.J. from the Civil War battlegrounds on the other side of the porch.

"P.J.!" I warned. I 'd been sure he was in another century. Children have the most amazing selective listening skills.

"It's okay, Peej," said Heather. "I'm not really a lesbian. But I'd have the guts to be one if I wanted to be." Huh? What does Heather mean with comments like that?

P.J. nodded and went back to war.

Date:   Thursday, August 13, 2:35 P.M. EDT
From:   SwimSlave
To:       Wanderlust
Subj:    Early Morning

I woke up just before 3 A.M. As I focused on the fluorescent red numbers of my bedside clock, I calculated that if I got up right now, I'd have three full hours by myself before anyone else got up.

I sat on the floor of the porch, just drinking tea and listening to a screech owl. What an eerie, lonely sound. I wondered if it was calling out to another screech owl or just luxuriating in the sonata of sounds it could make all by itself. I thought about how nice it would be to have you sitting next to me.

I went back to sleep a few minutes before six, then woke up with the kids around 11:30. This could work.

Date:   Friday, August 14, 12:39 P.M. EDT
From:   SwimSlave
To:       Wanderlust
Subj:    Fun and Guilt

The shopping trip went well. Margot was torn between spending her school budget on swimwear and motivational books, or letting Chloe talk her into actual items of clothing, which Chloe would, of course, immediately try to borrow from her. P.J. was thrilled to find boy-sized silk boxers in a camouflage pattern. He wanted to buy one pair for each day of the week but I held my battle-line at two pairs.

Chloe was intent on buying chopsticks for her hair. She likes to start each school year with a fashion signature piece all her own, and then pretend to be outraged when the other girls copy her. So this year she plans on decorating chopsticks with designs rendered in nail polish and then poking them through various braids, buns, knobs, twists and other assorted hair protuberances. I am all for this chopstick idea if it will delay the inevitable journey towards body piercing.

I tried on a pair of khaki shorts and a matching blouse. "Mom, you really should think about integrating more color into your wardrobe," was P.J.'s advice. Margot said the shorts looked a little tight through the hips, and maybe I should try a larger size so I'd be more comfortable. Chloe added, "Mom, that look is just so *eighties*. By the way, your hairstyle needs major updating, too."

Date:   Saturday, August 15, 5:30 A.M. EDT
From:   SwimSlave
To:     Wanderlust
Subj:   Countdown

Even though you teased me by sending me *Deliverance,* I know how supportive you are about my trip, Thomas, and I want to thank you for that. Especially because last night was a very bad night. Pete decided to wait until the last possible moment to tell me he doesn't want me to go. He started in by saying that his parents are too old to watch our kids for the week. I reminded him that it was his idea to ask his parents to babysit. I reminded him that his parents are always complaining that they don't see enough of their grandchildren. I reminded him that it was too late to cancel and long past time to be talking about this. I reminded him that he didn't have to change a single thing in his own schedule other than to drive the kids to his parents' house on Sunday and to make sure the cat and the rabbits had food.

"What rabbits?" was Pete's surly response. "We don't own any rabbits." I just looked at him. "What rabbits?" he asked again. I simply did not have the energy to do the groveling it would take to convince Pete to feed them. So instead, I stood up wordlessly, picked up my pocketbook, and drove to the mall. I bought Rainbow and Star the biggest, fanciest, least-confining travel cage in the pet store. I charged it. With pleasure. Furthermore, I can't wait till Pete sees the bill, so don't even think about offering to reimburse me for it, Thomas. However, you *can* take me out to lunch sometime.

When I left the pet store, I went right to a fashionable sporting goods store and bought khaki shorts that fit better than the ones I tried on for the kids. I found a bright red sweatshirt and bought that too, for *integration*. Duly inspired, it occurred to me that I've been vaguely troubled about how I'll keep in touch with you from the wilderness, so I went to the computer store. I had an idea that I might buy myself a small notebook but the prices were staggering, almost as much as the cost of my high-priced wilderness excursion. Plus, without electricity, how would I recharge it? And I would need a phone line to actually mail anything.

Then, as I was sluggishly wandering the aisles for the second time, I stumbled upon the answer—a waterproof and supposedly indestructible word processor designed for school kids. It runs on three AA batteries and will hold up to 65 pages and can be plugged into a Mac or a PC so that the files can be downloaded when I get home. It was lime green with a little decal of an alien on it.

A salesperson approached, one of those superior-acting computer types with an assortment of pens in his chest pocket. Despite the pocket protector, one of his pens seemed to be leaking, causing what looked like a tiny black oil spill in the left lower corner of his pocket. I hoped he'd never heard of "Spray It Out".

I just knew this computer nerdclerk would try to make me feel inferior. And he did, making up for a lifetime of datelessness. He looked at me. He looked at the green thing in my hand, and curled his upper lip unattractively. I stammered something about this being for my youngest child, and was about to embellish my lie with a line about the child still being in diapers. He cut in to say that the item I was considering was a blender. No, that wasn't it. He said it was a *toaster*. I flashed him my phoniest smile and said, "Thank you, that's exactly what I was looking for."

Pete was asleep when I got home. He's still asleep now. I'm kind of wishing he'd stay asleep until after I leave.

Date:  Saturday, August 15, 9:30 A.M. EDT
From: SwimSlave
To:     Wanderlust
Subj:  Countdown Continued

Just got off the phone with Heather. She said to bring Rainbow and Star to her house and the little girl who lives next door who is feeding her goats will feed the rabbits too. Don't worry, I'll keep them in their new cage on her porch. They'll be safe. So don't give it another thought.

Date:  Saturday, August 15, 12:39 P.M. EDT
From: SwimSlave
To:     Wanderlust
Subj:  Countdown Continued Again

I was just wondering if there's any chance you might arrive while I'm gone. Is there?

Date: Saturday, August 15, 7:00 P.M. EDT
From: SwimSlave
To: Wanderlust
Subj: Countdown Still Continued

We just finished dinner and Pete is cleaning up while the kids are packing and I'm sneaking in to write to you. Pete is trying so hard to be agreeable that we barely make eye contact.

The good thing is that now I'm really looking forward to the trip. I know I could use a short "Special Delivery" away from here.

Date: Sunday, August 16, 3:20 A.M. EDT
From: SwimSlave
To: Wanderlust
Subj: Countdown Almost Over

I'm wide awake. I don't know what to expect. Promise me if you come back while I'm gone, you'll wait here until I get back? I'd really love to see you again, Thomas.

Heather is picking me up at 6:00. I'll write when I can and send it all the second I get back.

# Part 2

Date:  Saturday, August 22, 9:00 P.M. EDT
From:  SwimSlave
To:    Wanderlust
Subj:  A Week's Worth

Thomas, I've been home since late afternoon. I have been thinking of you, and want you to see that I wrote to you quite often, you might even say almost constantly, while I was on my "Special Delivery" trip. So, here it is. Attached as a file, I think that's the right way to say it, before I've even downloaded it to read myself. Does that mean it's still uploaded? With luck it's in order, just as I wrote it on my trusty little green machine.

SUN 8/16 APPROX. 10 P.M.:

HEATHER IS ASLEEP ON THE OTHER SIDE OF THE TENT BUT I WANT TO TELL YOU EVERYTHING, THOMAS,

BEFORE I FORGET ANY OF IT. THIS IS NOT AS EASY AS IT SOUNDS BECAUSE RIGHT NOW I AM VERY TIRED. I AM CURLED UP IN A SLEEPING BAG IN A DAMP, CALIGINOUS TENT WITH A FLASHLIGHT TUCKED INTO THE CROOK OF MY NECK. I FIND THAT I HAVE TO KEEP SHIFTING MY BODY AROUND JUST TO SEE THE KEYBOARD IN WHAT IS A RATHER CAPRICIOUS BEAM OF LIGHT AS THIS MACHINE DOES NOT HAVE ANY BACKLIGHTING OF ITS OWN. ALSO I CAN SEE ONLY FOUR DIM LINES AT A TIME, AND THOSE ONLY WHEN MY NECK DOESN'T CRAMP. I WOULD LIKE TO KILL THAT ASSHOLE FROM THE COMPUTER STORE FOR NOT EXPLAINING THE TERM TOASTER. TOASTER MEANS ALMOST OBSOLETE, AND NOT ONLY CAN I BARELY SEE WHAT I'M TYPING, BUT IT ALSO SEEMS AS THOUGH IT ONLY TOASTS IN UPPER CASE. OPTIMISTICALLY, THAT COULD BE A PROBLEM OF THE LIMITED LIGHT, NOT THE LIMITED MACHINE. I WILL LOOK MORE THOROUGHLY FOR A SHIFT KEY IN THE MORNING.

HEATHER PICKED ME UP THIS MORNING AT 6:20 WHICH IS ABOUT AS PUNCTUAL AS SHE GETS. SHE INSISTED ON DRIVING HER CAR WITH THAT BUMPER STICKER SO I SLUMPED DOWN LOW UNTIL WE WERE OUT OF TOWN. OUR INSTRUCTIONS WERE TO DRIVE TO LONG-TERM PARKING AT THE HINGHAM FERRY DOCK AND, IF YOU CAN BELIEVE IT, LOOK FOR A MAN CALLED hans. oh look, it does toast lower case. now where is that shift i need it for the question mark////z/a/q/? Okay, this isn't so bad after all, as long as I keep switching the flashlight from one shoulder to the other. Anyway, we park as directed and get out to look for Hans. The only possible Hans candidate is this absolutely gorgeous tall blond specimen dressed in a majestically cut chauffeur's uniform and leaning against the side of a long, white limousine. If I could find italics, as if this toaster might even have italics, I would italicize gorgeous and long, the former for Hans and the latter for the limo, although the reverse could work as well. Anyway, at this point Heather gives me a Heather look and says, "Told you this would be fun."

"You must be Hans," she gushes. And he is. He opens the rear door and out steps a woman who is one of the two owners of "Special Delivery". She is well past sixty and wears her age with some defiance. No makeup. Coarse grey hair in a crisp short cut that she probably doesn't even bother to blow-dry even when electricity is available, something that will horrify Heather if she thinks about it. And the kindest faded blue eyes, utterly surrounded by wrinkles. It looks as if a flock of crows have landed and walked around those eyes. I like her immediately. She shakes both of our hands with the firmness I expect and introduces herself as Maude Dufresne.

"Welcome to 'Special Delivery'. Please put these on after you're seated comfortably." And, with that, Maude hands Heather and me each a black satin blindfold, the kind of eye covering that is softly edged in lace and advertised for beauty sleep.

"Does Hans wear one, too?" asks Heather teasingly, with this sexy, provocative lilt to her voice. Maude and Hans laugh companionably, as do the two women who are already seated in the limousine, wearing satin blinders identical to ours. The women seem somehow familiar, even blindfolded, as if I have seen them in the grocery store or at the doctor's office. I have the unsettling feeling that Heather and I would appear to them exactly the same way, as if we were all from the same approximate mold. I remember, just for a moment, when Margot was an infant and Pete and I had hired our first babysitter. After I explained to the sitter that we were just going to run out and see a movie and eat a quick dinner, she widened her eyes and dropped her jaw and said that, oh wow, we were the third couple she'd sat for that week while they did the same thing. Not just a movie and a restaurant. But that particular movie and that particular restaurant.

Maude explains that the rest of our party will meet us later. The blindfolds, she says, will help us to relax and also add to the feeling of adventure. Hans drives off and we can hear a soft mechanical purr as the sheet of tinted glass that separates him from us begins to rise, then stops when it connects quietly to the ceiling. I try to sense where Hans is taking us, to recognize the twists and turns of roads I know well. If my admittedly flawed sense of direction is accurate, we are heading for the middle of a very wet and deep ocean. I give up and lean my head against the sumptuous welcome of the leather seat.

We drive in silence for what is at least a few minutes and might be much longer. It is curious how being blind-folded changes your time perception. A stereo system begins to radiate soft New Age music. I recognize rain-forest sounds. Otherworldly sounds. Wet sounds. It is at first quite soothing but too soon all the running water makes me have to go to the bathroom. I wonder how long the limo ride will last and if there will be bathroom stops along the way and if so will we have to manage blindfolded? I plan to rebel enough to remove mine once inside the stall no matter what anyone tells me.

The rainforest music changes to monkish chanting. When I first notice a new smell in the car, I try to con-nect it thematically. I want to perceive it as the incense I remember from the earliest days of my childhood, when Mass was still sung in Latin. I picture the Monsignor in long flowing robes, importantly swinging the incense burner back and forth in a long trajectory as he paces the center aisle.

It doesn't work. The smell reminds me more of house-work. Of something I really hate. Furniture polish, that's it. The smell is lemon. Too strong for tea. Much more like dusting. Alerting rather than calming.

Our olfactory tour continues. Pumpkin pie spice. A meadow in springtime. The ocean after a storm. It's not unlike seeing a movie through your nose. It becomes increasingly soothing. Restful. Maybe I could nap for a bit.

Maude's voice breaks in gently. "My partner Millie Scott and I met five years ago when our husbands were being waked at the same funeral parlor. Several weeks later we nodded to each other at the town library. It was odd to think that someone could share your experience if not your pain. We nodded again at the grocery store. And one day, again at the library, we began to talk in a great big rush of words, as if we'd been saving up things to say to each other for years and years.

"Millie was already planning a trip to a dude ranch in Montana, and even though in my previous life I would never have considered going, I decided to join her. Next we went to The Grand Canyon, then Alaska, then Paris. Soon, women friends were asking us to take them along. It seemed they didn't quite have the nerve to do it alone. They wanted the adventure but not the responsibility of choreographing it, perhaps because so much of their lives was about taking care of other people's details. Millie and I found ourselves giving birth to 'Special Delivery'."

I am surprised that Heather hasn't made a single crack, like how she'd love to make friends at *her* husband's funeral. I figure she must be asleep but I can't be sure because my eyes are temporarily unavailable. The music drifts back. I recognize Bonnie Raitt, the song about running naked through the city streets and getting back to the fundamental things. I drift pleasantly through four or five songs from the same CD, thinking how Bonnie's mean slide guitar and bluesy voice have never sounded better.

My right side has gone numb, Thomas, so I'll say goodnight for now. I'll try to bring you up-to-date in the morning.

MONDAY, 8/17, FIRST LIGHT

I slept the sleep of exhaustion last night, waking up a couple of times, thinking for a minute about rolling over, deciding I was too tired, and returning to a heavy slumber. I'm not sure that I even registered that I was not in my own bed at home.

When I awoke this morning, it was still dark. I lay on my back with my knees bent and the soles of my feet pressed down to rest my back and waited for enough light to continue my chronicle. I am sitting now with my crossed legs tucked back under the sleeping bag. I'm sure the others will be up soon, although we haven't actually been told a thing about today's schedule. We were instructed only to relax and enjoy the week as it unfolds. So I will catch this up to the present as quickly as I can.

After Bonnie Raitt comes a bathroom stop. The limousine pulls right in front of a restroom door. To my immense relief we're allowed to remove our blindfolds before we debark. We all blink a few times and no one can resist a quick look around but as far as we can see we are pulled off the highway in Anywhere, USA. The other two women and I head straight for the stalls but Heather stops to ask a woman standing at the sink what town, state and country we are in. The woman, who I'm sure is startled by Heather's mascara-smudged raccoon eyes and disheveled hair and probably thinks she is an escaped convict, turns without answering or drying her hands and all but runs from the restroom. Heather howls with laughter. The other two women join in politely from their stalls.

Back in the limo. Another hour, maybe a little more, maybe a lot more. A blindfolded lunch that feels like eating in braille. The round, smooth thing is a grape. Maneuver it to your mouth. The rectangular, dense thing is cheese. . . . More music, classical this time.

And then we arrive. The limo stops. The doors are opened. We remove our blindfolds and look around. Vast woods on three sides. Directly in front of us is a huge lake over which an enormous hot-pink ball of sun is beginning to set. Between us and the lake are five large wooden canoes, painted hunter green. Hans begins to unload the trunk, Maude directs us in helping him and Heather cracks, "How are you going to row all five of those at once, Hans?" Heather is getting on my nerves already. I can feel her trying to ruin this for the rest of us. Hans just laughs and everyone else ignores her.

As we're walking back and forth between the limo and the canoes, another vehicle, identical to ours, pulls in. The driver steps out first, a tall and black and beautiful man with the most magnificent smile even though he is missing one front tooth. His earlobes have been cut and the lower part of each stretches halfway to his shoulder. Maude introduces him to us, saying that he is a Masai warrior here from Kenya as a Ph.D. candidate at Harvard and likes to be called Biff. Biff adds that in his country both his missing tooth and long earlobes are marks of beauty that would allow him to take all of us as his wives at once. We giggle appreciatively but apprehensively.

So this is the rest of it: Biff opens the other limo. We meet Millie who is tiny and delicate with her hair in a long grey French twist. She reminds me a little of Ruth Gordon in "Harold and Maude". (I do know that movie titles should be italicized, but I don't have any italics. Wait, I can do it like this: HAROLD AND MAUDE. That's better.) I like Millie right away. There are four women in the other limo, too. Introductions all around. We are assigned two to a canoe into which is packed every- thing we will need for a week. We wave good-bye to Hans and Biff. We paddle across the lake until our arms and shoulders burn, until we think we'll never make it. But we do. We drag the canoes well up onto the sand of a pretty little beach and quickly set up the tents in a clearing just beyond the sand.

Heather chooses me as a tentmate. We throw our stuff into the tent, grab flashlights, and join the others at a campfire that is already burning. We pass around shrimp cocktail and gourmet pasta and vegetable salad that Millie and Maude produce from a thermal bag. We each drink a single glass of dry champagne, the last alcohol that will be available on the trip, we are told. Heather moans loudly. Millie reads something beautiful about living in the moment, but I am too tired to notice who she says wrote it. We say goodnight and return to our tents. Heather says, "Whose idea was this anyway?" and falls asleep almost immediately. I think I will too but instead find myself up for hours writing to you. I feel like I am somewhere apart from time and place and still connected only to you.

Heather's up and I don't want her to see this.

MONDAY, 8/17 AFTER BREAKFAST

Breakfast this morning consists of Mueslix and yogurt consumed around a campfire that is heating the water for coffee and tea. We are told that the yogurt will be our last item requiring refrigeration and, in fact, it is nearly room temperature already, although I'm sure it spent the evening packed in a thermal cooler. Fortunately, there is a recently invented cream for coffee that does not require refrigeration, although unfortunately it is half and half and not the two percent I prefer.

After we stacked our breakfast dishes and sat back down with a second cup of coffee, Maude said, "It is our grand hope that there will be a special experience for each of you over the course of the next week. Call it what you will—an epiphany, a manifestation, a breakthrough, a revelation.

"Just after Millie and I started 'Special Delivery', I was sorting through some dusty old notebooks and I came across a line I had transcribed in college, 'dea incessu patuit', which is from Virgil. It means 'and she revealed herself to be a goddess', as Venus did before Aeneas. Millie and I invite you this week to find your goddess within, the part of you that makes you uniquely *you,* and will set you on a path of personal growth and fulfillment. This week, we hope each of you will reveal yourself to be a goddess. And you will announce to the group, or possibly the group will announce to you, 'dea incessu patuit'. Please say it with me now."

"Dea incessu patuit," we chant. I notice that Heather, seated next to me, doesn't join in.

Our assignment this morning: to explore our environment ALONE (a paper-bag lunch provided) and come back when we feel that we can draw a meaningful map of our surroundings.

## MONDAY, 8/17 LATE AFTERNOON

Thomas, we're on an island! I walked the entire circumference, which must have been at least two miles. There are just a few sections that could pass for beach, none as imposing as the one we're camped near, and as I think about it, perhaps the sand on our beach was brought in by boat. The island is on a lake. I am sure now that it is a large lake and not the ocean even though there is a billow, not quite a chop, to the water that makes me think of the sea. I have tasted the water and there is not a trace of salt. It sounds silly, I'm sure, but I am so proud of myself for thinking of tasting the water. I only hope that I have not ingested e-coli bacteria.

In non-beach sections, the trees grow right up to the edge of the water. I was able to identify scrub pine and oak. There also are lots of jutting rocks and some adorable wild blueberry bushes, shorter and rounder that the domesticated varieties. Most, but not all, of the blueberries are gone or maybe have just been eaten by the birds, but I sampled a few of the stragglers and they were delicious. I felt quite brave eating them before double checking with Millie and Maude that they are in fact blueberries and not something capable of killing me in a ghastly and excruciating way.

Back at the campsite, I join Alex and Helen, the two women who rode in my limo. Everybody else—Traci, Kate, Mary Paige, Heather and Betsy—trickle in to start creating their maps. We work on large sheets of beige newsprint paper with brightly colored markers. I have never tried to draw a map before. I have always resisted giving directions in writing, too, as if I will somehow be held responsible if the other person gets lost. But this map is fun. We are drawing our vision of the island, I think. And when we have finished, we hang the maps with wooden clothespins, the old-fashioned kind without the spring, on a clothesline stretched between two pines. The maps crinkle in a gentle breeze as we all sit back to appreciate their harmony.

Next, Millie produces an enormous roll of toilet paper, the largest I have ever seen. I experience relief tinged with a pinch of embarrassment that we are finally going to discuss bathroom protocol. Or lack-of-bathroom protocol. I have already used most of my only pack of travel tissues, which I have responsibly buried when soiled by kicking a hole in the soft humus-y soil with the toe of my shoe and then covering it back over and tamping down the soil with my foot. The sight of tiny Millie with her elegant French twist and her diminutive, almost Lilliputian, bearing, holding a mammoth role of toilet paper, makes us all smile. She smiles back. An "isn't this all so much fun" kind of smile. "Please pass this around, my lovies, taking just what you'll need for today's activities."

Some of us take a little, some a lot. I take just what I think I will need, so that I don't appear greedy, so that I don't look like a person who wastes paper and doesn't recycle, and just in case this roll is all the toilet paper we have for the week. The roll circles back to Maude, who tears off just a couple of sheets and hands it to Millie, who does the same and then places the rest of the roll on a tray in front of her. "This," Millie says, gesturing to the still large roll of toilet paper on the tray, "is one hundred percent biodegradable and will break down along with your valuable human waste products to fertilize this lovely island. We ask only that you bury the evidence."

"These," Millie continues, waving her own sparse collection of paper squares with a sweet smile, "are for now. For each square you possess, you will tell the group one thing about yourself." A groan goes up from the group, loudest among those who have wrapped the paper around their hands like gauze around an injury. I think of that famous SEINFELD episode. Elaine and another woman in rest room stalls, Elaine without toilet paper. She begs plaintively but the woman next to her refuses to "spare a square".

Am I boring you with this, Thomas? I realize that I am sometimes writing more to myself than to you, and yet it is the need to communicate with you that keeps me writing or at least I think it is. Although I have to admit that I enjoy this writing even when I forget all about you. My point, I guess, is that you should feel free to skim over the parts that don't interest you.

Anyway, I promise I won't tell you every word of what everyone said. Especially because some of it could make you uncomfortable. I don't know if you are aware of this, Thomas, but when a group of women gets together, much of what they laugh about is at the expense of the men in their lives. What I have to admit to you, and I really hope you won't hold it against me, is that even though I think some of it is mean, and even though I would never, I don't think, tell stories like that myself, some of the stories are very, very funny. Mary Paige told us about a time when she complained to her husband that he never wanted to do anything socially anymore. She said, "Just tell me. What do you like? What do you want to do?" And her husband said, "I used to like it when we had whole families come over for cookouts. The kids and adults would all play volleyball or baseball in the yard and everyone would take turns holding each other's babies. I really liked that."

"But, honey," his wife answered. "Nobody has any babies anymore. The kids are all grown up. They don't want to be with us anymore. They have their own lives." I mean, here is this guy whose kids are gone or almost gone and he's waiting around for a cookout with toddlers. Well, it sounded funny when she told it.

Helen told us that when her husband comes home from work, he sits at a table across from her with a drink in his hand, and drones on about how he said this to that person and that to this person and really showed them all. She said that while he tells these stories and she oohs and aahs with feigned interest, she fantasizes about leaping across the table at him and strangling him until his eyes bulge out and he shuts the fuck up. Her words. Anyway, maybe it was the way she told it that made it funny because it's not really writing that funny. By the way, Thomas, I know how different you are from the men in these stories. So much more sensitive and aware.

Okay, so I'll just tell you one more part. The most interesting things were said by someone named Traci (I just know she spells it with an "i". Probably dotted with a smiley face.) Traci is the youngest of the group, somewhere in her late twenties or early thirties. She stands out as the sole orphan among the rest of us, who really are a solid, well-maintained, creeping-toward-the-other-side-of-mid-life-and-hoping-to-laugh-about-it sort of a group. Traci has a wraithlike quality not fully explained by the fact that she looks like she weighs about two pounds and must be close to ten feet tall. She has fine, expensively dyed blonde hair and big vulnerable brown eyes and is fully made up over her tanning booth tan. She just doesn't seem to be someone who would go on a trip like this. She looks too much the Barbie Doll, as if her arches wouldn't flatten out to fit into hiking boots.

Traci tears off a square of toilet paper. The first thing she tells us is that she only took a couple of squares because she gets constipated every time her boyfriend leaves her. She looks around the circle at the small sea of sympathetic faces and bursts into tears. She sobs quietly and squeaks when she draws in a deep breath. We wait, not wanting to intrude.

Traci tears off another square, wipes at her tears and then crumples the wet paper in her hand. She tells us that she is a makeup artist for a Boston film company that produces rock videos. Every time her boyfriend leaves she cries all over the clients and misses a lot of work, so her boss, who is like a big sister and a friend of Maude's, paid for Traci's "Special Delivery" week. Her boss thinks it will be easier for Traci not to go back with Donny if she is unavailable for a week. Traci, who looks good even with tears, who has not yet arrived at the age when crying causes ugly swelling and lasting puffiness, holds up her third and final square. "And I am never ever ever going back to Donny Lawson because he is an asshole and I deserve better."

This is it and we know it. Our first goddess. "Dea incessu patuit," we chant spontaneously. Betsy and Alex run off to pick wildflowers to tuck into Traci's hair and we all, even Heather, escort her around the beach in a kind of laughing procession. It feels good.

Have to go because it's dinnertime. I'm ravenous.

Monday, 8/17, WHILE HEATHER SLEEPS

When we first signed up for "Special Delivery", along with our packing information, we received instructions to bring a few gifts in specific categories. Tonight we each presented a gift to nature. I planted a dozen daffodil bulbs. They're supposed to be white with apricot centers, a variety called "Beautiful Dreamer". I know it's early to plant fall bulbs but they should be okay. I love the idea of leaving behind some evidence that I had the guts for this adventure. Maybe I'll carve my initials on a tree, too. And then maybe someday we can row here together, Thomas, and you can carve yours right beside mine.

Tuesday, 8/18, BEFORE LUNCH

This morning is mostly free time. Millie and Maude set up a rope hammock between two trees. They suspend a shroud of mosquito netting from a high branch. Millie is extremely agile for her age and it is a delight to watch her scamper up a tree. Maude remains on the ground, working quickly and efficiently until the netting envelopes the hammock in a cloud. This they encircle with a dozen or so citronella candles in little aluminum buckets. It has an altarlike effect. Our assignment is to take a turn spending about a half hour in the hammock just "being".

I walk around the island, feeling like I should be DOING SOMETHING, until I see that the hammock is vacant. I lift up the netting and climb underneath. I remember that I always like being in a hammock once I actually get settled there, but the climbing in is so awkward that I tend to avoid the whole experience. The netting helps by creating a subtle camouflage. I think that perhaps I'll set up an arrangement like this at home when I return but Pete's voice breaks into my daydream. "What the hell is this supposed to be?" I shake my head a few times until the voice dissipates. I do not want his opinion.

Do you like hammocks, Thomas? This one IS comfortable. I try to keep my mind clear, but as soon as it empties, an image rushes in. I am in a rerun of GILLIGAN'S ISLAND. I try to decide if I am Ginger or Mary Ann. In the long run, is it better to be sultry and sexy or perky and peppy? Ginger looks good now, but Mary Ann will probably age better. Plus she will have developed her personality in a way that Ginger won't feel the need to. But Ginger DOES get all the men. And the good clothes. And you certainly never see her doing any real work. She'd never risk breaking a nail. I decide that women have just talked themselves into thinking they'd prefer to be Mary Ann. We'd all really rather be Ginger.

I see a couple of women chatting at the far end of the beach, politely waiting a turn in the hammock. Heather is one of them and it occurs to me that if she's here, then I could be enjoying our tent all to myself. I flip my legs over so that they're hanging off the side of the hammock and then just kind of propel myself forward. The momentum takes me to a standing position. I decide that maybe I've just always been too tentative before. I think this might not only be true about hammocks but about most of my life.

I wish I didn't have to ramble on without a reply from you. What I wouldn't give for some electricity and a phone line and a computer to plug my trusty little toaster into. Then I could send this along and read all of the e-mail that I'm sure you've left waiting for me. (Other than that, I don't miss civilization at all.)

Tuesday, 8/18, BEFORE DINNER

After lunch, we trek to a clearing at the center of the island, a place I have not discovered in my explorations. It does not appear that this is a natural clearing. Stumps of various heights and diameters, separated from each other by random distances, stand at attention. Under my sneakers, the pine needle floor feels thicker and softer than in other parts of the island. I think you would enjoy this, Thomas, because I bet you're a lot more daring than I am, but all I can think of is that this is the sort of thing I would let Pete try with the kids while I found a good book to read.

Glancing up, and I mean WAY up, Thomas, I see a thick metal cable stretched between two trees, one on either side of the widest part of the clearing. From the center of this cable a shorter piece of cable hangs by a loop. A thick piece of rope is draped over a pulley attached to the other end of this vertical cable. Both sides of the rope touch the ground, and the excess rope is coiled neatly on the ground. My guess is that I am about to discover a whole new category of things I am terrified of, requiring a kind of physical daring I have never developed.

With very little preamble, and some quick reassurance by Millie that she and Maude have been trained by both "Outward Bound" and "Project Adventure", we begin a series of trust falls. Maude shows us how to stand in two lines facing each other. We learn to "zipper" our forearms so that we create a human safety net.

Both feet planted firmly on the ground, Millie crosses her hands over her chest, stiffens her body, and turns her back to our blanket of arms. Maude is our coach as we recite the following—Millie: "Ready to fall." Us: "Ready to catch." Millie: "Falling." Us: "Fall away, Millie."

Millie leans back, we hear a tiny plop and she is in our arms. Then Maude, some forty or so pounds heavier than tiny Millie, takes a turn, and though the sound when we catch her is more of a thud than a plop, catching Maude when she falls is not much harder than catching Millie.

Of course, we are all expected to take a turn. I think it will be easier to be the last, that I will learn by watching the others. Betsy and Helen jump right up and do it easily, Alex is shaky but determined, the others are all somewhere in between. When it is finally my turn, I find that even though I am able to lace my arms across my chest and hold my body rigid, I am simply unable to let go. Although I know a safe tapestry of hands is waiting just inches away to catch me, somehow I cannot quite will my body past the point where I am spatially in control. The harder I try the less likely it seems that I will succeed. It is in some way like trying to be spontaneous. Or like trying too hard not to try so hard.

Maude is standing directly behind me. If I am ever actually able to fall, she will catch my head. The others keep their hands zippered, but Maude moves her hands in to lightly hold my back, and I go through the whole drill, the cueing and answering, without in fact falling. Instead, Maude eases me down to reach the other hands.

We repeat the exercise several times, and each time Maude moves her hands back, maybe inches, maybe only fractions. I am a diapered infant learning to walk, a six-year-old with blue lips shivering at the edge of the diving board. Warm maternal voices encourage me along every step of my journey. I am surprised by the power of this group. I think I would try anything just to thank them. Finally, I land in their arms with the resolute sound the others have made. I wonder if I am having a harder time than the other women trusting the group, but then I realize that my hesitation has more to do with not trusting myself.

Maude moves the group to a tree stump, wide and sturdy, maybe a foot off the ground. She asks me to be first this time. I want to say no, thank you, truly I've had enough. I've learned enough for one day. Obediently, however, I climb up. My voice shakes when I call out, "Ready to fall". And somehow I do. Amazingly, I discover it's not much harder to fall from a height, that you just have to take a deep breath and forget about how silly you must look, and once you do, the momentum carries you to your destination. I wonder if this is a profound thought or something everyone but me has always known.

I work my way up, stump by stump, to a height of about four feet. Then it is my turn to encourage the others. I am an energetic and caring coach. When it is

Heather's turn, she immediately climbs the highest stump. Turning her back to us and crossing her arms over her chest, she yells, "I think I'm a goner, Doc," and hurls herself into our arms without giving the proper cues. Millie takes her aside for a private talk.

We take a break to eat granola bars and drink green tea from adult-sized juice boxes. Millie and Heather come back and Millie tells us about our next challenge: "The Flying Goddess". Oh shit.

We are each supplied with a 30-foot length of rope and given lessons on how to tie a harness called a "Studebaker". It is really fun, like being a Boy Scout finally, since my childhood Girl Scout troop would never let us do knots. The only distraction is Heather, who just can't seem to stop making comments about bondage, and being glad to finally learn something useful. Although, Thomas, I have to say, I'm not really sure what you could actually DO in this harness, without giving the other person rope burns.

Anyway this is how to tie a "Studebaker", Thomas, in case you ever want to know. Although, just in case you ever really DO need to know, please double check with a professional before you climb or fly in it, just in case I don't have it all exactly right.

Okay, so what you do is fold the rope in half and put the midpoint at the center of your back. Tie it in the front by crossing one side over the other and looping it through. Pass both ends through your legs from front to back. Reach around to the back, grab both ropes, and pull them to the front. Pass the ends toward the center of your body, under the V at the front. Pull the ropes taut as you squat to insure a tight fit. (I think at this point a man would want to be especially careful, Thomas.)

Then make a tie at the back of your waist exactly like the one you made initially in the front. Pass both ropes through your legs again but this time from back to front. Reach around to the front, grab both ropes and pull them to the back. You're going to do just what you did in the front and pass the ends toward the center of your body under the V of the rope, but it will be harder this time since you can't see what you're doing. So, my advice would be to imagine you are wearing a skimpy string thong because that will help you find the location of the V. And just relax and feel around and you'll be able to figure out where to put the rope ends.

Then squat again and kind of wiggle around a little and pull the ropes as tightly as you can even if it gets uncomfortable down there because you have to remember that eventually you'll be traveling in this "Studebaker". Oh, I get it. That's why they call it a "Studebaker". Sorry, you probably knew all along—the harness must be named after a vehicle because it's the only thing you're going to be riding in up there, and I mean WAY up there.

Then bring the ends to the front and make another tie at the waist. Wrap the excess around once and then bring what's left to one side. Make a square knot and reinforce it on both sides with a bowline knot. (Someone of your worldliness and experience most likely knows these knots, Thomas, but if not, I'd be happy to provide further instructions.)

We make an engaging picture, this group of mostly middle-aged women tied up in rope harnesses in the middle of a pine clearing in the middle of a lake in the middle of nowhere.

I watch numbly as Maude straps on a helmet. Millie hooks the shorter end of the rope to the back of her "Studebaker" with a large metal clasp called a carabiner. As Maude waits calmly, Millie lines us all up along the longer end of the rope. It seems that if we pull back on our end, we can make Maude fly. This feels like more power than I want or need.

Nobody asks my opinion nor do I volunteer it. And we do make Maude fly, up some fifty feet or so in the air. And then, eventually, it is my turn to try. What the hell, I think, I'm so overwhelmed already, what's a little more trust, a little more growth?

The hardest part is that, once the cueing is finished—"Ready to fly . . . Ready to lift . . . Flying now . . . Fly away, Beth!"—I have to turn and run away from the group as they lift, in order to get a good swing going. Once again, I fear that last split second when I can still stop, still hold back.

I am determined. "One, two, three . . ." I say to myself. "Four, five, six . . ." I add when my legs refuse to work. "No!" I think. I will not be stuck here on the ground. And I turn and run. Hard. After about the sixth or seventh step I find myself still running, my legs circling around and around but no longer touching the ground. I know I have seen some cartoon character do this on Saturday mornings and I make a mental note to ask P.J. who it is when and if I make it home.

When I look down, I am carsick. Given that I am wearing a "Studebaker", I think this is very, very funny. I laugh with great big gulping noises that I have never heard before. Tears are streaming down my face. It could be the wind or the altitude but I think it is mostly fear and excitement. I stretch my arms out wide to the sides. I bend one knee to the front and extend the other out high in the back, in what we called a stag leap when I was a junior high cheerleader. Oh my God, I suddenly remember being a cheerleader.

You should see the harness bruises I have now, Thomas, and in the most amazing places. But nobody said it would be easy.

Wednesday, 8/19, VERY EARLY AND NOT MUCH SUN

It is so dark in the tent this morning that I have to squint to see the keyboard. The air is swollen with moisture and I can hear the mosquitoes sniffing at the tent seams. Last night was a blast. We gave each other pedicures by candlelight and Traci did our makeup. She gave us slices of cucumber to place over our eyes while we waited for our turn with her. We created quite a tableau—a row of women in the wilderness with freshly painted toes, all semi-reclining and blinded by pieces of salad. Traci knows lots of tricks for what she calls the "effects of time and face".

In fact, Traci has an amazingly original use of language. Some of it is just trendy. She says things like "starter marriage" for first marriage and "McMansion" for those brand new oversized colonials that are deforesting New England. But as she was showing me how to even out my skin tone by applying a ghastly shade of green underbase, as if I'd ever take the time to do all that in real life, she started to sneeze repeatedly. I asked her politely if she thought it was a cold or an allergy. She said she thought it was stress and it was ruining her life so she was "trying that euthanasia stuff". I had an immediate image of Traci on a Dr. Jack Kervorkian wait list until I realized that she thought she was saying "echinacea".

I hope the weather is better wherever you are, Thomas. Will I ever hear from you again? I wish there was some way to check e-mail from here.

## Wednesday, 8/19, MIDMORNING

It is muggy and buggy and starting to sprinkle and Heather is crawling the tent walls. I meant that figuratively but maybe I should suggest that she literally try it for something to do besides telling me how bored she is.

## Wednesday, 8/19, LATE MORNING

I attempted a short walk to get away from Heather. When I came back, she was trying to read my letters to you! She said (again) that she was just bored, she wasn't really trying to snoop and what was the big deal? Why was I so upset? We had a very big fight. I may have overreacted, but HOW DARE SHE touch my personal things? She's stormed off somewhere and I'm the happier for it.

I've been wondering about how it is that I have stayed friends with Heather all these years. It just occurred to me that once I started dating boys, I may have stopped valuing my female friends. I called them only when I didn't have anything better to do, then less and less until the friendships just drifted away. Even after I got married, my friends weren't really my friends at all but half of a matched set. The wife of one of Pete's friends, the mother of one of my kids' friends. Heather is still my friend simply because she is the only one who kept calling me.

## Wednesday, 8/19, AFTER LUNCH

We all squeezed under a tarpaulin that has replaced the hammock, at least for this drizzly day. We had a lunch of almond butter and marmalade sandwiches with warm seltzer. Everyone was trying not to be grouchy but the weather certainly made me miss my air-conditioning. Even a small fan would seem a luxury right now. Heather showed up with Traci, very buddy buddy. Traci's roommate, Kate, seems to have hooked up with the two women, Alex and Helen, who rode in our limousine. It was a relief to go back to the tent alone for a few hours of solitude before dinner. I think I'll nap now.

## Wednesday, 8/19, BAD NIGHT

Tonight was just awful. And right now Heather is behaving like a martyr, pulling her sleeping bag up over her head as if she is bothered by my tiny beam of flashlight, a light that I certainly do need if I'm going to write to you. As if I haven't put up with every sort of bad behavior from her for years and years. I have just remembered that she even stole my sixth-grade boyfriend, Jerry Springer. No, not Springer, but something close to that. I'll think of it in a minute. But no way am I going to turn off my Itsy Bitsy light just to let Queen Heather get her beauty sleep. I think I'll stay up and read for a while.

## Thursday, 8/20, BEFORE HEATHER GETS UP

Last night was like a bad dream. After dinner we all huddled in the damp around the campfire. We each placed a citronella candle behind us, hoping to surround ourselves with protective flame, but the mosquitoes were tiny vampires determined to find blood. Although Millie and Maude seemed intent on remaining cheery, it was becoming a stretch for the rest of us. Wine would have been nice. Our activity for the evening was to each give a gift to the group. Our registration information had prepared us for this assignment. We had been encouraged to think not necessarily in terms of material things and to be creative.

Alex began by drawing quick pastel sketches of each of us. The drawings were merely okay, although we all oohed and aahed over them. We promised to frame and hang them as soon as we got home, even though they were already beginning to smudge from the moisture in the air.

Traci seemed quiet and withdrawn but managed to pass around a small box filled with temporary tattoos and to help us apply them on what she called our "erroneous zones"—the outside of an ankle, the back of a shoulder, over a cheekbone. My unremarkable cheek was quite improved, I thought, when I saw it in the mirror festooned with a black rose.

It was my turn next, Thomas, and I have to tell you how difficult this kind of thing is for me. I always think I've come up with a great idea, until just before time to present it, and then I'm wracked with second-guessing and self-doubt. Am I being redundant? Are second-guessing and self-doubt the same thing? Anyway, sitting in the safety of my home, I had thought it would be so much fun to tell everyone's fortune. So I packed a gypsy scarf and some great big silver hoop earrings. I also packed a book I'd found called POCKET PALMISTRY, which I'd skimmed before leaving, and really meant to get back to before tonight.

Pretty much all I had time to read before dinner was about how to make "hand maps". I realized, too late, that I should have brought an inkpad and paper with me. My newfound island resourcefulness was with me, though, because I immediately thought about bringing everyone down to the damp sand on the beach to make handprints there. We ran down to the edge of the water like a bunch of teenagers. I instructed everyone to press both palms into the sand, and then to remove them carefully. I tried to sound like an ancient Indian sage while I said, "The hand must have four fingers and one thumb, and if there are any more, or less, it is a very bad sign."

In the same voice, I told everyone to look at their palm prints, and if the fingers were wide apart and resembled a starfish, the mind was quick and flexible. If the fingers were close together, the mind was closed and conventional. If the little finger and ring finger were separated, you were free in your actions. If the middle finger was separated from the fingers surrounding it, then you were an independent thinker.

This last part made everyone laugh so I thought it was a good place to end. I hope I gave everyone accurate information because this is a group that would appreciate these kinds of details for clues to self-knowledge.

Next, Kate gave out these cute little wooden massagers. They fit in the palm of your hand and looked like toy beetles with round balls at the end of the feet. We all turned to the right and massaged each other's backs with them. We giggled a lot and it felt amazingly good.

And then Heather. I am tempted to leave this story out because of the subject matter, but since I've detailed everything else that has happened so far, I'll try to control my embarrassment. I can't think of a delicate way to tell you what Heather did. I guess I'll have to just say it. Heather passed out heavy cotton dinner napkins to each of us and began a lesson on how to fold them. I can't speak for the rest of the group but I was certainly expecting something I could use at a dinner party. An origami-like fan or a swan or maybe just something abstractly simple and elegant. But as we all followed

Heather like lambs to our slaughter, what gradually appeared was a cloth growth that rose with each fold of the fabric until it was unmistakably a fully erect and rather substantial penis.

Can you believe it? And of course, Heather couldn't stop there but had to continue to shock by telling us she would now share her heretofore secret and guaranteed effective blow job techniques. At that point she launched into a demonstration of fellatio, alternating garbled, cloth-obstructed murmuring with exaggerated male moans and declarations of undying love and fidelity.

A sudden torrential downpour was the fitting end to Heather's performance. We all raced to our tents. As we pushed back our tent flap, Heather was still laughing her head off. I told her flat out how unbecoming her demonstration had been, which only made her laugh harder.

And now, this morning is still damp and bleak and the end of our week of self-knowledge seems far, far away.

Thursday, 8/20, MIDMORNING

I left for breakfast before Heather woke up and when I returned to the tent she was up and gone. Just as well. The sky has cleared and our assignment for the day is to walk around with a sketchbook and colored pencils, and find something in nature that expresses who we are. Then we're to draw it and write about it. I wonder what I'll decide on. Fortunately for Heather, there are any number of phallic shapes from which to choose.

Thursday, 8/20, EMERGENCY!

Thomas! Heather and Traci are gone! We discovered it at dinner. A canoe is missing and so are they!

Thursday, 8/20, EMERGENCY CONTINUED

It is only an hour or two before dark, and though we've walked around the island, there is no sign of them in any direction. Millie has used the cell phone to call the police.

Thursday, 8/20, EMERGENCY FURTHER CONTINUED

It is almost dark. A boat from the lake patrol, carrying a local policeman, has just left. He said that they found the canoe on the mainland shore of the lake, less than a mile from the nearest roadway. He said there was "no evidence of any wrongdoing" and thus no reason for the police to look for Heather and Traci. He said that chances are someone gave them a ride into town and they're having a great old time. He was not very understanding. In fact he acted as if we were interrupting more important work. Probably he was just finishing his dinner or polishing his gun. Millie phoned Hans at home and he is on his way. I think I'll go back to the campfire and wait with the group.

Thursday, 8/20, LATE

We wait and wait around the campfire, little bursts of talk surrounded by long firelit silences. We start telling stories just to pass the time. Trips we've taken, that sort of thing. Maude asks if any of us have a goddess experience we'd like to talk about and one of the women, Mary Paige, who I've barely spoken to during the week, raises her hand, smiles a big toothy smile, and announces she has something to share.

Mary is striking in a vivacious kind of way. Great posture, good eye contact. Self-confident. Expensive hair and nails. I wonder if I've been avoiding her because she looks too good. Mary Paige's story is about how she has lied to her husband almost all of the twenty-three years of their marriage. It wasn't until they were married that she realized that money meant something very different to each of them. He thought her a frivolous spender, she thought him a tightwad. It wasn't a big problem until she stopped working to have children.

Every month her husband would open up the household checkbook statement and grill her about $100 here and $200 dollars there. He never looked at the checks themselves, just the check register in Mary Paige's handwriting and the statement with dollar amounts next to the check numbers. One day, after curbing her spending with difficulty for most of the month, Mary Paige tried an experiment. She recorded a scarf for $45 at Talbot's as a check for $45 worth of groceries at Stop and Shop. It worked. Food, it seemed, would not be questioned.

Before long, she was pretending to shop at as many as three grocery stores a week, and talking a lot about how lucky the boys were to eat such staggering amounts of food while remaining fit and trim. Her husband was gone often enough on business for this to work. When she wanted something that cost more money than a grocery check could cover, she would add on to this basic strategy. Once she pretended to adopt a Christian Children's orphan. Another time she faked needing periodontal work that their dental insurance didn't cover. In order to pay for her "Special Delivery" week, Mary Paige had feigned taking Masters' level courses at a nearby university for almost a year.

Mary Paige finishes her story by saying, "And this is my 'dea incessu patuit'. I have no intention of actually confessing to my husband or anything, I mean, let's be real here. But I think from now on I'll be the goddess of writing checks for any damn thing I want. And if he has a problem with that, then he'll have to figure out what to do."

I am astonished by Mary Paige's secret spending. Wouldn't it have been easier just to get a job while the kids were in school? I wonder if I should tell her about quotation work. I decide it's not my business. Maybe we all need to find our own way.

Hans calls once from the cell phone in the limo, saying that he has spoken to the police and is on his way to the nearest town to check bars and motels. He promises to call as soon as he has something more. We've all agreed to go looking ourselves in the morning. Traci's roommate, Kate, offers to let me share her tent and I decline politely. To be honest, as much as I'm anxious about Heather and Traci, it's nice to have the tent to myself. Maybe I should be more worried, maybe I'm only pretending to be concerned, but all I can really picture is that Heather and Traci are out dancing and drinking with the locals, while we're all sick with worry.

### Friday, 8/21, BEFORE FIRST LIGHT

Maude just came to my tent by flashlight. I think I heard her whisper "Beth?" immediately. I was sleeping the way I slept when my children were infants, one ear alert to any sound that didn't quite belong. I was always amazed that Pete could sleep through our babies' cries. Was it because he was confident that I'd be the one to wake up? If I had been elsewhere, would his subconscious know that he was on duty, that the life of a helpless being might depend on how lightly or heavily he slept?

Oh, sorry, Thomas. You're probably wondering why Maude was at my tent. She said that Hans had located Heather and Traci. When I asked for more details, she said she'd tell us all at breakfast, together, as soon as the group had gathered.

After Maude left, I sat on my sleeping bag with my eyes closed, just feeling the tranquillity of being all by myself. A phrase from an old Eagles song popped into my head about having a peaceful, easy feeling. I was thinking that I would miss this aloneness, not just when Heather came back, but when I returned home. I had a fleeting image of pitching a tent in our backyard, and just disappearing into it when the need for solitude became too much. Immediately the tent vision filled with the rest of my family. "Beth, what the hell are you doing in there? Can we come in too, Mom? Mom, what's for dinner?"

Oh my God, I just realized I've hardly thought of my family at all this whole week. Immediately I feel a powerful surge of the guilt I had felt before leaving them. Aah, that's better. This I recognize.

Friday, 8/21, AFTER BREAKFAST

Listen to this, Thomas. I mean, just listen to this. We meet at the campfire as the sun is rising, although the spectacular orange streaking of the sky is all but lost on us. We wait for the news politely and anxiously.

Millie stirs a big pot of Cream of Wheat laced with golden raisins and honey over the fire. Maude walks around our circle pouring coffee for each of us. Finally, we are all sitting around the fire with heavy white cereal bowls balanced on our laps and mugs of strong coffee (to which chicory has been added the way the French do) on the ground in front of us, and Millie and Maude repeat the story that Hans has phoned them.

It seems that Heather got the idea to run away, or I guess it would be row away, yesterday because she was bored and Traci wanted to call Donny and knew Millie and Maude would never let her borrow the phone. Heather figured she'd talk Traci out of calling Donny once they found a town but in the meantime Traci would be a motivated traveling companion. That is just so Heather.

Heather and Traci simply paddled and paddled in what seemed to be a straight line until they came to land. They pulled the canoe up onto the bank, slung their pocketbooks over their shoulders, and walked to an occupied lake house. They knocked on the door and made the man who answered laugh by politely asking if he would mind calling them a cab. Instead, after informing them that he couldn't even guess where the nearest cab company was located, he drove them to the only nearby town, which of course had only one restaurant.

By then, Heather had invited the man to join them for dinner. We all grinned when Millie said that, Thomas, but she didn't smile back. Apparently, Millie continued, Heather forgot all about talking Traci out of calling Donny, so when Traci excused herself to go to the bathroom, Heather didn't suspect that she was secretly calling him. Traci returned to the table. They drank wine and more wine with their dinner. All of a sudden, Traci burst into tears, and told Heather and their new friend that she had not only called Donny but told him where she was. He had hung up on her so she wasn't sure if he was ever going to speak to her again or if he was on his way to find her, which was starting to feel like not such a good idea because Donny was known for his violent temper.

At this point, the new friend should probably have driven them to the nearest motel, wished them luck, and excused himself. But instead he invited them back to his house for safekeeping.

Millie didn't give us many details about the next stretch of time but I, for one, certainly had a picture in my mind. Heather would have forgotten about Traci by now. She would be working on making this man find her more attractive than Traci. Heather would have done this whether or not she was in any way attracted to him. It would have been a point of ego. Heather is always testing to see if she still has it. IT being, I guess, the ability to attract anything with a penis.

When they got to the house, Heather may or may not have gone off to the bedroom with this stranger. I know what I'd guess.

However it came to be, Traci was asleep alone in the tiny guest room just inside the front entrance when Donny showed up. One of the waitresses at the restaurant told him not only who the woman fitting Traci's description had left with but also how to get to the man's house. Guess there's not much else to do in these little towns but to notice things like that. When Donny found the house the door wasn't even locked. Maybe Traci half-wanted him to find her. But she surely couldn't have wanted what happened next.

I stared at my hands folded tightly in my lap, as Millie told us that Donny grabbed Traci by her hair while she was sleeping. I stole a peek at Kate across the circle, but her eyes were closed. Millie continued the story and I imagined Traci just waking up when Donny yanked her out of bed and flung her into the opposite wall. I could feel her terror as the impact dislodged a mirror from the wall over her head, and fractured her skull. Pieces of glass pierced her right cheek and her collarbone, Thomas. And when Heather and their host came running into the room, Donny was angrily kicking Traci in the thighs and abdomen while screaming at her to wake the fuck up, goddammit.

With rather cinematic aplomb, Hans burst in at that very moment. Millie didn't give us the details about that either, but I can picture Hans, elegant in his chauffeur cap and uniform, telling Donny to stop with such quiet authority that he just stopped. Do you think that's how it happened, Thomas, or was it more dramatic than that? Maybe Hans had a gun. I like to think he didn't need one though.

The lake house owner called the ambulance first and then the police. Heather held Traci's hand while Hans guarded Donny. The police arrived and took Donny away in handcuffs. Heather and the man drove behind the ambulance while Hans rode in it with Traci. I am so glad Heather didn't get to ride with her. She certainly didn't deserve to.

The rest of their night was spent waiting to hear the extent of Traci's injuries and giving statements to the police. As Millie reached this point in the story, we were all holding our breath. I felt both relief and horror when she finished by saying, "Traci regained consciousness on the way to the hospital. There does not appear to be any brain damage. She has several broken ribs and will need plastic surgery for lacerations on her face." I was not the only one to grimace at the thought of damage to Traci's angelic face.

"Who will take care of her?" asked Kate. She had drawn her eyebrows in toward each other with a concentrated squint. She looked as if the entire incident had somehow been her fault, as if it was her job to take better care of Traci. I am beginning to notice how much time women spend, with notable exceptions like Heather, borrowing guilt that isn't theirs.

Maude answered her soothingly. "Hans and Heather will stay with Traci until her boss arrives. Her boss, Jan, is one of my oldest and dearest friends and she adores Traci like a daughter. Traci will move in with Jan. Jan will take care of her while she heals and make sure she has a job to go back to. Jan will see to it that Traci gets counseling. She has already agreed to testify against Donny."

"Don't you just hate it," said Kate. "That someone as sweet and smart and gorgeous as Traci would go back to an asshole like that?"

"It's because she thinks she can change him," Alex said. "It's romantic to think you can change a frog to a prince, an asshole to a non-asshole. He's probably really nice after he beats the shit out of her."

"Yeah, she wants to take care of him, to help him get better," Mary Paige said, shaking her head.

"Let's call him up right now," Helen said. "We'll take care of him."

Well, we didn't really call him up, of course, Thomas. But what I'd love to hear from you is the male perspective on Traci's story. Why do smart women, who know better, keep going back for more abuse?

"Is Heather coming back?" I was so glad that I didn't have to ask that question, that Alex asked it first and in a tone not much nicer than the one I would have used.

I was amazed that Millie's face didn't reveal judgment. "Heather has not been invited to spend the last evening of our "Special Delivery" week. Hans will be canoeing back with Heather shortly to pick up her things." Millie's eyes sought mine across the circle. "Hans will come back in the morning to drive Beth home in the limousine."

Maude spoke next, as if by prearranged signal. "When Heather arrives, you may choose to interact with her or not. But remember, Heather will be carrying the memory of last night for the rest of her life."

A less polite group might have groaned in unison. Instead, some of the women began to clear away our breakfast dishes, others poured another cup of coffee. I glanced over at the lake and saw a canoe in the distance. I decided to take a long, slow walk around the island.

I trace the route I followed on the map-making excursion back when it was all uncharted territory. Was that really less than a week ago? The island feels snug and cozy to me now. I turn and walk inland, scuffing a path in the pine needles so I can find my way back, until I'm surrounded by trees. The sun sends polka dots of light through the spaces in the scraggly oaks and scrub pines. I remember the conservation land that borders my house and how I rarely set foot in there.

I think about the daffodils I planted on this island and plan a trip back in the spring to visit them. I picture myself renting a canoe, hoisting it onto the back of the car single-handedly (or maybe you can come with me, Thomas), driving up to wherever we are. . . . At this point, I interrupt my reverie to wonder if we'll drive home blindfolded now or if we'll be allowed to look.

When I return to my tent, all signs of Heather are erased.

Friday, 8/21, LATE AFTERNOON

After lunch I find myself back in my tent, spacious without Heather's jumble of clothing and magazines. I curl up on top of my sleeping bag and wonder how Traci is doing. How does someone like Traci end up with someone like Donny, a bully and a brute? How did I end up with Pete, the nice guy, the good father? How did you end up with Cindi, Thomas? How did you end up without her?

I remember Traci talking about working on a video shoot with a large group of extras. The director paired them off into couples. As Traci was touching up their makeup, she found out there was a real couple in the group, who told her that in all their years of acting, not once had they ever been matched up by a director. "I guess opposites detract," was Traci's explanation.

What is the gap in Traci's self-esteem that makes her think she deserves someone who has hurt her before, may even hurt her again? Is it something her parents didn't tell her, some bit of love they didn't give her? I think of my own three children. Have I covered all the self-esteem bases? Have I bully-proofed my children? Would they know enough to walk away from a Donny if he entered their lives? Have they been too sheltered? In our quest to keep them safe, have Pete and I protected them too much? Would they be so unfamiliar with danger, they'd fail to perceive it if it sought them out?

Friday, 8/21, LATE LATE

My keyboarding skills have improved this week. My fingers are absolutely flying over the keys of this lean, mean, green machine. Tonight was the perfect final evening. After a dinner of grilled summer vegetables skewered on sticks of bamboo and served over a bed of couscous flavored with fresh cilantro, we chatted around the campfire for a few minutes and then moved down to the beach.

Millie and Maude gave us each a pencil and a pad of Post-its®, not the flags I use to mark quotations but the larger squares for writing notes. I chose that wonderful rich shade of Post-it®-purple, too deep for lilac or lavender but lighter than the royal hues of purple. We were urged to write one of our faults on each square and to keep going until we ran out of time. Well, I was whipping through that pad like I was being paid by the word. I started out with the nagging little faults and just kept digging deeper and deeper until I uncovered some major problems, including lack of focus and sporadic bursts of anger at my children. Before I knew it, Millie was telling us time is up, lovies.

Millie and Maude pair us up, their six remaining charges. I am placed with Betsy, a woman I've talked with just a few times during the week. Our assignment is to find a surface where we can stick our notes vertically in two side-by-side columns. It is rather intimidating to see one's faults displayed on the side of a scrub oak tree for all the world to see. I quickly shuffle mine, mixing up the trivial and the important items so that nothing seems either too superficial or overwhelming.

I start to read Betsy's list (on yellow squares) and I am amazed at the similarities. She says she needs more direction in her life, wishes she could be a better mother, was less controlling. I continue to read. Why, she has fat thighs, too. I never would have known. She disguises them well. I wish I'd paid more attention to her outfits during the week.

Maude breaks in to tell us that we must now take turns singing our lists loudly and with great gusto to each other. I go first. And here it is, Thomas, my faults, some of which I may delete before I send this to you:

I am too controlling, though not actually a control freak. (I have to take a deep breath before I finish the second part of the phrase. Without really planning to, I seem to be singing to the tune of "Here Comes Peter Cottontail".)

I start things without finishing them.

My house is only fake clean.

I have fat thighs. (I've already mentioned this.)

My hair is very grey. (Although the color is now its authentic former color and not some fabricated shade. Maybe I'll take this one out, too.)

I don't always listen when the other person is speaking.

Sometimes when I am alone I watch soap operas and eat most of a box of rich chocolate cookies that I would never let my kids eat. (This one works pretty well with "Peter Cottontail".)

I sometimes judge people based on the town they live in.

Betsy, whose voice is flat and scratchy and even worse that mine, takes her turn, with a tune that I think may be "Take Me Out to the Ball Game" and we are both laughing hard by the time she's finished. Next, Millie tells us that we have to choreograph a dance to go with our combined songs and we should both chime in on the shared faults. We come up with a great little chorus-kick for the fat thighs' line. And by the time we perform for the whole group, it's hard to take anyone's faults too seriously, which I suppose is the point.

Maude pulls out a shopping bag filled with feather boas, fake fur stoles, and big rectangles of netting dotted with rhinestones. I've always wanted to wear a black feather boa but never thought I was the type. Tonight I'm the type for anything fun. We parade up and down the strip of beach, singing silly songs at the top of our lungs, a group of women getting older and looking forward instead of back.

Right now, I'm sitting here thinking that I can't believe this is the last night. I feel like knocking on one of the other tents and starting a pillow fight.

Saturday, 8/22, 4:00 A.M.

I know it's 4:00 A.M. because I just rummaged around in the dark to find my watch. Tonight I had a very strange dream. How could my mind, even my subconscious mind, invent something like this?

In my dream I am reclining in a hammock made of men's silk ties tied together in a kind of macramé fashion. I can feel both the slippery softness of the longer lengths of tie, as well as the pressure of the hard knots through the gaps in my clothing. I notice that I am wearing only a kind of long flowing gown made entirely of bird feathers. I can feel individual feathers blow to a standing position, leaving minuscule bits of my skin exposed to the air. I am not at all worried about how much of my body is laid bare.

I look down and notice the peacock feathers and how they contrast nicely with the seagull feathers (bleached a pure white for both aesthetic and sanitary reasons) on one side and the grackle feathers on the other. Vibrant red-winged blackbird feathers are surrounded by the quieter colors of wren and sparrow. The longer I look, the more I see that my outfit is a vast and infinite repetition of pattern and depth.

I begin to be aware that my dream has some sort of siren motif. In my downy suit, I appear to be all softness and fluff, and yet because a siren's looks are so deceiving, underneath I am a temptress, an enchantress, a seductress. Because in my waking life I often mix up sirens and mermaids, in my dream I look down to check my feet, just to make sure I'm not wearing fins. My feet are intact, my toenails have been painted a color I've never seen before and therefore cannot identify by name, to which flecks of real gold have been added like glitter. In between each toe has been placed a daisy, which tickles.

I'm relieved not to be a mermaid because I'm enjoying the siren motif. I glance around me and am not at all surprised to see Scylla, Homer's famously dangerous rock from THE ODYSSEY, jutting out of the water. Just as casually I look the other way and notice that the whirlpool, Charybdis, is right where it should be. I sigh, content that I am waiting at the end of this perilous passage in exactly the spot where a good siren should be.

But wait. One of my daisies is moving and when I look down I see that this is not going to be a purely classical dream. Someone is freshening the flowers between my toes and he is certainly not Odysseus. There is nothing about him that speaks of the ravages of sun and sea.

It is a young man at my feet, a perfect Greek god of a young man. He is tall and lean, with clearly defined muscles under bronzed, oiled skin. His eyes are blue and his hair is black and full and long. Oddly, he is wearing only a white cotton garment that is somehow a cross between a loincloth and a diaper. His left ear is pierced with a large safety pin, a smaller pin pierces his right nipple. As he twists around to pick another daisy from the garden that grows conveniently just beyond my hammock, I see that there is a small key protruding from a lock at the center of his back. It reminds me of the Tressy doll of my childhood, the one whose hair would get longer when you turned the key. I wonder for a moment what will happen if I turn the key before me now.

Traci's voice, unattached to any body but clearly Traci's voice, interrupts my thoughts: "He's a boy toy, Beth, a boy toy."

"Are you sure, Traci?" I ask. "But what does he do? Tell me, Traci, what does he DO?"

As this bronzed demigod watches, I reach one hand down along my stomach and under the waistband on my white cotton underpants. I am surprised that I'm not wearing better underwear. I rest the heel of my hand on my pelvis as my fingers explore the moistness around my clitoris. Quietly I circle my hand around just a few times until the waves of orgasm begin under my fingers and radiate downward toward my toes. Wow, I think in my dream. This boy toy stuff sure works fast.

This is the bravest dream I've ever had, Thomas, and I just had to tell someone about it. It's hardly something

I'd talk about around the campfire at breakfast, and it's not a story I'd bring home to Pete. We don't talk about sex, although we used to have a fair amount of it in the good old days of our marriage. And I have never in my life talked about masturbation to anyone but my children, and then only to say to them those are your private parts. If you want to touch them, it is something to be done privately. It is such a baby boomer parent thing, to be open with our children about sexuality, when all the while we're barely able to say those words to ourselves.

I remember when Margot was first asking me, "What's this? What's that?" And I would answer elbow and knee. And I remember feeling so superior to my own parents because when I was changing her diaper and she asked what's this, I didn't slap her hand away or say that's your pee-pee. I found a mirror the way they suggested in OUR BODIES, OURSELVES. Which, by the way, I found out that while this might be necessary for adults, it's not for toddlers because they are very flexible and can see everything they need to see without a mirror. Anyway, I named for Margot all of the parts that I was sure about. And she learned the words right away the way she learned every new word.

Months later the pediatrician removed her diaper as part of her regular checkup. She looked down at herself and said, "vulva!" in a happy, singsongy voice as if delighted at recognizing an old friend. I felt my face turn scarlet with embarrassment. The pediatrician raised an eyebrow and said, "It's okay. My wife drives a Volvo, too. A green one." I never quite knew whether he was trying to make me feel better or worse.

I never told anyone the vulva story. I kept it buried underneath layers of embarrassment until it resurfaced in the middle of this dark island night on the tail of a dream.

Do you know that my time in the tent without Heather is the only time I've been alone overnight for as far back as I can remember? There is always someone with me at night—if the kids are away, say at camp, Pete is in the house; when Pete goes away on business, the kids are home.

Saturday, 8/22 10 A.M.

Oh, Thomas, I've just finished saying good-bye to the island. The tents are dismantled and everything's packed but my trusty toaster. I've already decided that I'm going to wear my blindfold on the ride home even if Maude and Millie tell us we don't need to. I want only to relax in the limo and block out the rest of the world until the last possible moment. It's hard to believe but I'll be home by late afternoon.

Date:   Saturday, August 22, 4:30 P.M. EDT
From:   SwimSlave

To:     Wanderlust
Subj:   Home Again

It's so wonderful to be home again. I missed my full-size keyboard. And it was nice to have an e-mail waiting from you. Thanks for telling me you're looking forward to hearing all about my island adventure. I was a little disappointed that you still didn't mention your arrival date. I hope it's not far off.

I probably should take the time to edit the attached file before I send it to you but I'm in a rush. Pete and I are going out to dinner, just the two of us.

Date:   Saturday, August 22, 4:40 P.M. EDT
From:   SwimSlave
To:     Wanderlust
Subj:   Hmmm

On second thought, I really should have edited the absolute *volumes* I wrote to you during my "Special Delivery" week. Oh well, too late. Could you just skip over any parts you hate?

Pete is in the shower now so I'll tell you about my home-coming. As Hans and I turned off the road and headed up our driveway, we could see P.J., dressed in full cam-ouflage gear and carrying a plastic rifle, partially hidden behind a tree. Just when I was going to ask Hans to stop the limo so P.J. could ride the rest of the way with us, he disappeared. We inched along, alert to possible ambush, and soon I was able to show Hans the nose of P.J.'s gun sticking out behind an overgrown scrub pine near the house.

P.J. jumped out from behind the tree, peppered the limo with imaginary gunfire, and yelled, "Mom's home!" The screen door banged open and before I knew it, P.J., Margot, Chloe and Pete were all hugging and kissing me at once. Inside, pink and green crepe paper streamers crisscrossed the kitchen and a great big poster-board sign read, "Welcome Home, Mom!" A lopsided cake sat on the kitchen counter, repeating the sentiment in M&M writing on bright green food-color-dyed frosting.

Other than the cake, there didn't appear to be much in the way of food left in the house. Another time, that might have bothered me, but not today. The kids and I just piled into the car and headed out to the grocery store. We forgot all about nutrition and swim training and just put one of everything we liked in the cart. I remembered that when the kids were younger, a favorite game was to spend a Sunday morning cutting out coupons for unhealthy food. When we got to the store as soon as it opened at noon, they would each get a cart and a small share of coupons. If they could match the proper weight and variety and all the rest of it to the coupon, we would buy the item. Today it takes no time at all to fill our single cart. Surprisingly, there are a couple of exotic melons and some mesclun lettuce and lots of seltzer mixed in with the chips and cookies and candy. They really are growing up, these kids of mine.

I can hear the shower turning off in the bathroom, Thomas, so I'll say good-bye now. I'm planning to spend some leisurely time enjoying my family so don't be surprised if you don't hear from me for a few days.

Date:    Sunday, August 23, 3:49 A.M. EDT
From:   SwimSlave
To:       Wanderlust
Subj:    SO ANGRY, SO HURT

So much for my marriage. And it started out to be such a promising evening. When the kids were curled up with pizza and a movie, Pete and I headed off on what felt like a date. We had a lovely dinner at a restaurant we'd never gone to before, complete with eye contact and conversation. We were both clearly trying to get along and it seemed as if we'd discovered a secret: both of us were making an effort at the same time.

After dinner, Pete opened the car door on my side for me and suggested we go out dancing. I was thinking about how much my week away had changed Pete, how much more attentive he was, and that things between us would be better now. I wasn't quite ready to swoon but it was nice. We went to the Driftwaye, the only local place we could think of that has dancing on

Saturday nights. We hadn't been for years but it felt just the same. The band was playing the kind of music that makes you think you're at someone's wedding.

We found an empty round table waiting for us some distance from the crowded dance floor. We ordered wine and I excused myself. You'd think after a week of roughing it, I wouldn't have noticed but I was appalled at the condition of the rest room. Carefully, I layered long strips of toilet paper over the seat to protect myself from bathroom-borne diseases. I was remembering Millie holding the giant roll of toilet paper on the island and thinking how much fun I'd had. How much less tentative and afraid I felt there, how much more willing I was to take risks in my life.

I returned to the table. Pete and I sipped our wine and smiled at each other. When the band started playing "Heat Wave" (Martha Reeves & the Vandellas), Pete raised his eyebrows. I nodded and we got up to dance. We wove our way to the dance floor, Pete walking behind me the whole way. We danced playfully, taking turns spinning around in front of each other, sometimes even holding hands. We kept dancing when the band started playing "The Heat is On".

"Why don't we do this more often?" Pete whispered in my ear when we moved into each other's arms for "Hot Fun in the Summertime". We finished the dance and Pete followed me back to our table.

143

A woman approached us. I wondered if she was going to tell us what a lovely couple we made. She leaned close to my ear. I couldn't hear a word she was saying.

"What?" I asked.

"I'm sorry to have to tell you this but I think you should know you have a tail of toilet paper hanging, um, behind you."

Pete and I fought the whole ride home. I didn't see it, he said. If you still looked at me, you would have, I said. A husband who loves his wife would be watching her ass on the way to the dance floor.

"And, come to think of it, you only asked me about my trip once and that was a vague, 'So, how was your trip, honey?' and when I started to tell you about it, your eyes kept wandering over to the TV. When the news-caster changed, you said, 'Wait one second, Beth, I want to hear it. I just have to catch the sports first.'"

"It's always about what you want, isn't it, Beth?"

Date:   Sunday, August 23, 9:31 A.M. EDT
From:   SwimSlave
To:     Wanderlust
Subj:   Sadly

Pete and I are not speaking. He is out mowing the lawn. I think he is showing me how hard he works while I, by contrast, do nothing but gallivant off to islands. I'm having a hard time settling back into our routine. It feels like reentry into another galaxy. The oxygen needs are different and I'm floating several feet above the floors. I think I'll run out and buy bagels. Maybe that will feel familiar.

Date:   Sunday, August 23, 11:18 A.M. EDT
From:  SwimSlave
To:      Wanderlust
Subj:   Thanks, Thomas

Thank you for the e-mail, Thomas. And thanks for saying it but I don't really think I'll laugh about the toilet paper story someday. Are you laughing about things with Cindi yet?

You didn't mention it but I hope you don't think I've forgotten about the bunnies, Thomas. I promise I'll go get them later today. I simply can't deal with Heather yet.

Date:   Sunday, August 23, 4:10 P.M. EDT
From:  SwimSlave
To:      Wanderlust
Subj:   Guess Who?

Guess who just showed up uninvited? Heather! And under the guise of returning the rabbits, no less. She's downstairs now with Pete, sipping white wine while he drinks a beer.

They barely acknowledged me when I came in. And you know what Heather was wearing? Around her neck? A necklace with *feathers*! Heather was wearing a deep green tank top to set off her (newly) auburn hair. And I have to admit that the necklace, which consisted of tiny carved beads strung along a black leather string and separating some quite wonderful feathers, looked spectacular on her. Goldfinch, I think, the yellow feathers were. And something brown and fluffy. And another kind of feather that must have been from some kind of tropical bird with teal markings. I had a sudden vision of a row of disparate, miscellaneous birds perched along a telephone wire, cawing and tweeting about the bald spots caused by Heather's necklace.

I know it's impossible, but when I saw that necklace, my first thought was that she somehow knew about the dream I had on the island and was making fun of me for it. I got all flustered and had to pretend to have something to do just so I could sneak up here and take a few deep breaths. Don't worry, I'm better now. Maybe Heather's feather necklace had nothing to do with me, maybe she learned something on our trip, too. Maybe her island experience taught her how many wonderful wardrobe accessories can be found in nature.

I guess I should get back down there now before they miss me. Yeah, right.

You'd think Pete might have offered *me* a glass of wine. But no, he was too busy listening to all of Heather's "Special Delivery" stories. Heather's version was about as far from my own as you can possibly imagine. Not that Pete has heard my version.

Heather was merciless. She ripped apart the entire week, made fun of everything from the games and campfires to the other women. Pete hung on to every word, laughing and laughing at Heather's parodies. I wanted to say, stop, that's me you're laughing at. I'm the one you're feeling superior to. But maybe that was the point.

Heather left, finally. Sunday dinner was cooling on the dining room table by then, the meal that was my welcome home really, the meal that I was going to tell my "Special Delivery" stories over, the stories that no one would want to hear now. Pete was standing in the driveway, talking to Heather right next to that ridiculous bumper sticker.

I couldn't stand it anymore so I picked up Rainbow and Star in their fancy cage, slamming the door as loudly as I could when I left the kitchen. I placed the cage under the hutch, opened the door, and reached in to pat first one set of soft bunny ears and then the other. They looked up at me trustingly. Loyally.

Five minutes into dinner and the kids were doing all the talking. Pete cleared his throat. "So, Beth, when are you going to tell us all about your big week?"

As soon as you stop patronizing me, I didn't say. As soon as you stop being fascinated by my ex-bestfriend. As soon as you ask me a question that you'd really like to hear the answer to. As soon as you start looking at my ass again.

I looked around the table at my family. At my three independent kids and my husband who no longer loved me.

Date:    Monday, August 24, 2:18 A.M. EDT
From:   SwimSlave
To:       Wanderlust
Subj:    Dea incessu patuit!

Just a few minutes ago I felt my way into the family room and turned the computer on in the dark. I waited, thinking someone might hear the small electronic ping that signals the start-up. But, no, I am invisible here.

The computer screen glows warmly in front of me. I check my e-mail. My heart double beats in accompaniment as I search for Wanderlust, the one thing I have left to look forward to. Nope. Disappointment flops around a couple of times in my stomach.

All is quiet. Not even the questionable sound of someone rolling over in a bed to wonder about. I really am invisible. Should I try to walk through a wall just to see if I can?

There are five pieces of mail in my box. Two are sex site come-ons. Click twice for a free blow job. I don't even bother to look at those any more. I'm no longer even fascinated by the pictures of women with superhuman breasts. Although there was a time I would look at them all, trying to figure out if they were all the same woman with different heads superimposed. And they would certainly be walking. You could never run with breasts that big. And where do they find bras? I think of that old Oprah show when she carted out pounds and pounds of fat in a wagon. Maybe she could do another wagon show using silicone. Do men find those pictures erotic, Thomas? Do you?

Two get-rich-quick scams. I check my horoscope but it's still yesterday's. I sit and decide to tell you why I am awake.

I found myself suddenly falling out of sleep just a little while ago. There was a song playing in my ears. The Beatles were singing about love having a nasty habit of disappearing overnight. And I thought, oh my God, I am having a genuine, authentic auditory hallucination. I mean, I can actually hear The Beatles. They sound good.

I lay there for most of the song, as if I were having my own private concert. I liked the idea of John, Paul, George and Ringo, as they used to be, all curled up at the foot of my bed. I was partly thinking that maybe I was going crazy, even though I didn't feel any different. But if you're going crazy, you'd be the last to know, right? And the other part of me was just listening to every single word. Hot salty tears rolled down my cheeks even though I didn't feel like I was crying. Not exactly.

When the song was just about to end, I got out of bed in the dark and followed the sound. I ended up in P.J.'s room. His earphones had slipped off his head, fallen to the floor, and dragged the tiny radio with them. The fall must have hit the volume switch. I leaned over and turned off the radio. I smoothed P.J.'s tawny hair back and kissed him on his forehead. I was a little disappointed. It was a bit like thinking you'd seen a miracle, and then finding out the burning bush hadn't self-ignited but had been lit by somebody's match.

Back sitting on the edge of my bed in the dark, I stared at the lump of covers over Pete. I'm looking through you, I thought, in an echo of The Beatles' song. I see a man who has nothing more to give to me. I see a marriage that is over.

And that's when it happened. Dea incessu patuit! A little delayed perhaps, this off-island revelation. But somehow I knew in that instant that I had become the goddess of my own new life.

It is as clear as a bell to me now, why I have been writing and writing to you, Thomas. Meeting you has made all the difference in my life, made me see how *much more* of the world is out there, how little I've been settling for. And I know what I must mean to you because of the way you listen to me, the way you send me presents. I know what we can be to each other. What we are to each other already. Why, I never really even talk to anyone but you anymore. Not about anything that really matters.

It was destiny that sent us crashing into each other at the library that day, inevitability that has kept us in touch all this time. Imagine what a romantic story this will make one day. I'm so happy, Thomas.

Do you know that I read in *The Boston Globe* that 63 percent of women fall in love outside their marriage, or maybe it was 36 percent, but anyway it was *a lot* of women. In the same article it said that women who came of age in the '60s and '70s are the first generation of women who expect to have sex within their marriage and who make other arrangements when they don't. Considering all that, I probably shouldn't feel the least bit guilty.

Date: Monday, August 24, 8:18 A.M. EDT
From: SwimSlave
To: Wanderlust
Subj: Oh, What a Beautiful Morning!

I woke up a new woman. I am strong. I am invincible. Why, I'm Helen Reddy.

Just kidding. It must have been all that Beatles music last night because my head is just swirling with quotations. I think I'll work for a few hours.

Date: Monday, August 24, 10:08 A.M. EDT
From: SwimSlave
To: Wanderlust
Subj: Oh, What an Even More Beautiful Morning!

An e-mail from you, Thomas! Now my day is absolutely perfect and the morning isn't even over yet. And I'm glad you think my attention is flattering, and what a beautiful line about it being enough to make a lonely homing pigeon take flight. Does that mean I'll see you soon?

I just noticed that the sweet autumn clematis is in bloom. I thought you might like to know. I'm sure you would be able to smell it from your house if you were there now. . . .

Heather called yesterday afternoon to invite us over to play with the goats. Us as in Pete and me and Pete and the kids and Pete and did I mention Pete? Great, she can have him, and I can have you. What a guilt-free kind of swap. In fact, maybe they've been having an affair for years. Good, they deserve each other.

Now the old Beth might have been bothered by my best friend moving in on my husband or possibly already being moved in. But the new Beth sees it as very convenient and she starts to hum the washing that man right outta my hair song. "What is that noise?" asked Heather.

"I'm just humming a happy little song, Heather. It would be a pleasure to see you and the goats. Why, I'm sure Pete will be beside himself with excitement."

"Beth, are you okay? You've been mad at me since the trip, haven't you? Listen, I just talked to Traci. She's staying at Jan's house now. I told her that you and I would drive up soon and bring lunch."

153

"What an attentive friend you are, Heather."

"Stop, Beth. Do you have any idea how awful I feel about Traci? How responsible?"

So I stopped. Not that I believed her for a minute.

And after dinner, we all climbed into Pete's car and drove to Heather's house. Her husband and daughters came out and, if I didn't know any better, I would have thought they were one big happy family. Just as if *you* didn't know better, you might think we were one, too.

And the goats. The goats were adorable! Jasmine has a way of running after Solange and getting so excited that she becomes airborne for a moment. The closest picture I can give you is when Bambi falls in love, becomes *twitterpated,* and starts taking those cute little leaps. That's how it looked. And it reminded me of when our kids were toddlers. Everything they did was so cute, so happy. When they weren't destroying everything in their path. Even though the goats have eaten most of the perennials in their path, how could you not forgive them?

Only Jasmine is show quality. Solange has a double nipple, which is considered an imperfection, but sure seemed to fascinate Pete. Maybe he just liked the way Heather said it. She flung back a lock of her hair and said *double nipple* in a way that made it sound provocative.

Date: Wednesday, August 26, 6:38 A.M. EDT
From: SwimSlave
To: Wanderlust
Subj: Hark, A Word or Two From You!

When I checked my e-mail, I just knew there would be something more from you. Of course, I always think there will be something more from you and usually there isn't. But this time there was!

So you really are coming, Thomas!

I'm too excited to write.

Date: Wednesday, August 26, 10:18 A.M. EDT
From: SwimSlave
To: Wanderlust
Subj: The Picture of Composure

I re-read your e-mail about a dozen more times, which didn't take very long since it is barely more than a paragraph. Not that I'm complaining. I'm sure it's hard for you to write, Thomas, with all the stress that you're under.

I *will* watch for your check for the lawn service in my mail. It was nice not to have to remind you about it this month. And I'd be happy to get a couple of estimates for painting the outside of your house. Early fall is the best time for a paint job. I hope this doesn't mean you're coming back to get your house ready only to sell it. But maybe that is the best thing. I couldn't exactly pack up and move across the street from my family, could I?

And the mediation date you mentioned. Is that like divorce court without the judge? It sounds so civil, so mature. I'll have to file that away for future reference, if you know what I mean. Anyway, if your mediation date is September 10, then that means it can be no more than fourteen days until we see each other again. Can it?

Date:  Thursday, August 27, 7:13 A.M. EDT
From:  SwimSlave
To:    Wanderlust
Subj:  Moonlight

Last night the moon was surrounded by an oval of wispy clouds. One piece of cloud reached across the face of the moon like a handlebar mustache. I wanted to reach up with my hands to wax and twist the ends. I've never kissed a man with a mustache before. Do you still have yours?

Date:  Friday, August 28, 4:13 P.M. EDT
From:  SwimSlave
To:    Wanderlust
Subj:  Thinking of You

A productive day spent getting the kids ready for school. School starts early this year, before Labor Day. It used to be that only happened in the warm parts of the country, I think. My children complain but I think they're ready to go back.

We buy college-ruled paper for the girls, wide-ruled for P.J.. New backpacks which, of course, they don't really need. Lunch at the Food Court at the mall. We all head off in different directions to make our selections and then bring our trays to a central table. Chloe starts trying to con one more outfit out of me but I resist, saying that their tastes always change after seeing what the other kids are wearing. She backs off easily.

We stop at the beach on the way home. Swimming starts next week, too, and even Margot hasn't done much in the way of exercise during the break. They're meeting swim friends to go for a run so that when the coach asks they can tell him they've been vigilant. P.J. and I dig a hole in the sand and he lines it with seaweed. I ask him what it is. "A hole with seaweed," he answers.

Date:   Saturday, August 29, 12:01 P.M. EDT
From:   SwimSlave
To:     Wanderlust
Subj:   New Do

Pete is out mowing the lawn now. He mows the lawn almost every day, just so he won't have to talk to me. I've been sitting on the porch listening to the drone of the engine and staring over at your house. I'm imagining what it would be like to glimpse you in the window. To feel the heat of your presence across the way.

Just came from the hairdresser. My hair always looks its best about two weeks after it's cut, so I thought the timing for your arrival would be right. I find myself planning like that. Thinking that if I cut the roses now, there will be an abundance of fresh new blooms waiting for you when you arrive.

And if I think this way, life is good. I am okay. More than ever, you are my something to look forward to.

The salon where I have my hair done hosts a never-ending detonation of stories. They explode like fireworks from all corners of the shop. A funny line from under the hairdryer, a romantic tale from over the sink. Today, a bride is having her hair done for her wedding. As gerbera daisies are being threaded through her curls, everyone has a story to tell. Monstrously awful weather at a wedding ceremony twenty-six years ago, a honeymoon suite from hell ten years ago.

I sit silent. My own stories are wrapped up tightly like the layers of tissue that protect my wedding dress. They seem so fragile to me. If I take them out too often they will crumble into meaningless fragments.

Date:   Sunday, August 30, 10:22 A.M. EDT
From:   SwimSlave

To:     Wanderlust
Subj:   Lady Di

Pete and the girls are downstairs, glued to the news reports about yet another anniversary of Lady Diana's death, which is tomorrow.

I think it is maybe not so sad to die when you are at the peak of being in love.

The clematis is at its finest today. It is a mass of fuzzy white stars and tendrils. I've never watched before to see how long this stage lasts. I notice things like this now, since my trip to the island. I appreciate you more and more, too, Thomas. I see how rare and magical our connection is.

Date:   Monday, August 31, 8:59 P.M. EDT
From:  SwimSlave
To:     Wanderlust
Subj:   The First Day of School

Every year I take a picture of all three kids on the first day of school, standing side by side in front of the house wearing their backpacks. The kids moan and groan but I think they like the tradition. Someday, when Margot goes off to college, perhaps, I'll have the photographs all framed in a collage. A college collage.

As soon as P.J.'s bus comes this morning, I pick up Heather because we're heading to the North Shore to visit Traci. I am driving because even though I really want to see Traci again, I feel that I need to let Heather know that she's not in charge now. In fact, I decide she'll only get to see Pete on the nights I'm with you. And I'm still working on how we can keep this future arrangement a secret from the kids. I'd hate to be responsible for disrupting their childhood.

We sip cappuccino at Brewed Moon while waiting for a picnic lunch to be packed by an efficient-looking waitress. We're not in any hurry because the trick is to wait for the rush hour traffic to wane before setting out anywhere in the direction of Boston or beyond.

I decide to take Route 128 to avoid Boston altogether. Heather disagrees. She insists we should take Route 3 and pick up the Tobin Bridge in Boston and follow Route 1 the whole way. How once rush hour is over, you just fly through the city, how silly it is to go around. I smile sweetly and sing along with Fiona Apple on the radio, the song about being careless with a delicate man. Something I of course would never do, Thomas, just in case you have been wondering. When we get to the split in Braintree, I stay left and get on 128, still communing with Fiona.

"Beth, I thought we were going the other way. What's wrong with you lately?"

Date:  Tuesday, September 1, 4:30 A.M. EDT
From:  SwimSlave

To:     Wanderlust
Subj:   Awake

Even though the swim season doesn't start until next week, I awoke with a start just a short time ago, thinking hurry or we'll be late. It was an unexpected gift to find time alone in a sleeping house wrapped in a blanket of ebony sky and festooned with a sparkling thread of stars. I made a cup of tea and sat on the porch stoop, gazing over at your house.

I count the days until you arrive with the daisies of my dream, plucking a flower from between my toes and sending each petal into the wind. He loves me, he loves me, he loves me. No more than seven or eight petals remain.

Date:  Tuesday, September 1, 9:32 A.M. EDT
From: SwimSlave
To:     Wanderlust
Subj:   Delete Last Message, Please

Oh my God! How incredibly embarrassing. I have no idea what possessed me to send my earlier message. It is certainly too early to speak of love, even though we *are* connecting to such a degree. I think I may have been overcome by a poetic moment.

Date:  Tuesday, September 1, 12:08 P.M. EDT
From: SwimSlave

161

To:     Wanderlust
Subj:   Feeling Better Now

I redeemed myself with a burst of productivity. I am getting bored with the same old quotation areas but I know that as soon as the company changes the topics, I'll start to miss the old ones. Life is like that, isn't it, Thomas?

Now, back to yesterday's story:

Eventually, Route 128 leads to Route 1. Eventually, also, somewhere around Topsfield, I think, Route 1 becomes a little road that leads to places like Ipswich and Hamilton. It's very pretty countryside, although no self-respecting South Shore resident would ever admit to preferring the North Shore, or vice versa.

The house where Traci's boss lives is extraordinary. It's set away from the road at the back of a field that was once a horse farm. The house is big and modern and sprawling and of no style that you could ever find in an architecture book. The windows are the most striking detail. They're tilted, more than just a bit, and at the oddest angles. It must drive the neighbors crazy to see a house with crooked windows, but surprisingly, I like the way it looks. Whimsical is the word I keep thinking of. The trim around each window is painted a different color, teal or purple or pink or gold, and because the house is shingled in a traditional New England cedar, the effect is subtler than it sounds and actually quite nice.

Playful is the theme, and it continues throughout the interior. I think I told you that Jan (Traci's boss) owns a video production company, and it doesn't take me long to figure out where she keeps the props she isn't using. Every room is done in the style of a different decade. The kitchen is all 1950s, chrome and Naugahyde table and chairs, and a starched ruffled apron hanging from the knob of a cabinet door. I smell cookies even though none are baking, and expect Donna Reed to pop her head through the swinging half-door at any moment to pour us some milk to go with them. I wonder if our happiness would have lasted longer if my family and I had lived here.

The living room, where Traci is reclining on a black leather couch propped up by white leather pillows, is all eighties. Freestanding sections of architectural columns serve as glass-topped table bases. White walls, white carpeting, black bookcases. The only bit of color in the whole room is a red silk rose in a vase on an over-sized painting on the wall. I try on the idea of living like this, a glamorous and solitary kind of life without toys to trip on, other people's needs to consider. It feels too cold in here for me to thrive.

But it is not until I excuse myself to use the bathroom that I find my favorite place in the house. The guest bathroom is enormous and is set up like a cross between a sixties' beauty parlor and a barber shop, complete with two barber chairs facing a huge mirror, and what must have been the twin to the first beauty parlor hairdryer I ever saw. I am immediately transported to my first haircut.

I am in the second grade, and until now, my mother has always trimmed my thick, almost waist-length mane of brown hair. Short hair is suddenly in style for the first time in my short life and I am onto the trend. "I want to get a 'pixie' right away," I announce to my mother one day after school.

For whatever reason, most likely so that she won't have to listen to me screech when she combs out my long tangles, she agrees. The shop she takes me to is the closest thing our town has to a hair salon. It is really a barber shop but there are pictures of Twiggy and Twiggy look-alikes with their little boy hair on one wall.

The barber's wife is a hairdresser and has been to New York and therefore knows what is in style. I sit in a chair just like the one in Jan's bathroom. "I want a 'pixie', please," I repeat bravely. The barber's wife braids my long hair and cuts it off whole in a couple of squeezes of the scissors. It sounds like she's sawing through rope. She hands my braid to me. It looks like the tail of a dead animal.

I close my eyes and when I open them, I have straight-across short bangs and I notice my ears for the first time in my life. I see that they are shaped like my father's ears, only smaller.

I am not sure how it happens but somehow cutting my hair makes my eyes get bigger. They are as round as the polka dots on my favorite dress, the navy and white dress with short, puffy sleeves and a tie that pulls the waist in tightly and makes a big bow in the back over a flouncy full skirt. The barber's wife holds a mirror up behind my head so I can see the back view. "This will look great with a turtleneck," she comments to my mother in a knowing way.

"What's a turtle neck?" I ask, not really afraid yet. My mother points to a picture on the wall. I don't see a turtle neck. I see a lady model with short hair and a human neck. Definitely. "Where?" I ask.

"There," they answer, pointing in tandem.

I scrunch up my eyes but I still don't see it. "I think we'll get her one before we even go home," my mother says.

"But I don't want a turtle's neck!" I yell to myself in the mirror. The big round eyes have tears in them. I picture my neck being exchanged in some bloody, painful operation for a crepey reptilian neck.

"Silly," my mother says to me. "I think she's afraid it will hurt," explains my mother to the barber's wife.

"They don't hurt at all once they're on," the barber's wife tells me. "The only time you might feel it is when it's going over your head."

Over my head? I am terrified by the thought of all that gore touching my eyes, my nose, my mouth. "I don't want a turtle's neck! I don't want a turtle's neck!" I sob all the way home, even after my mother and I stop to buy a red cotton turtleneck which I refuse to wear.

"Beth? Are you okay in there?" Heather is banging loudly on the bathroom door. I tell her I'm fine and I'll be right out. But, even as an adult, I seem to be missing some key detail, something I should have known all along. Despite my recent growth, the feeling reappears. I wonder, before I leave the bathroom to join Heather and Traci, what I am not seeing now.

Date: Tuesday, September 1, 1:49 P.M. EDT
From: SwimSlave
To: Wanderlust
Subj: Heather Banging

Sorry, Thomas. Just as I was writing to you about Heather banging on the bathroom door, I could hear someone banging on the door in my own house. I guess I panicked and hit the *Send* button.

Somehow I thought it would be Heather at the door. Instead, it was one of the painters I called to get an estimate for your house. As I took the piece of paper he handed me, I told him that you'd be here in about a week and would call him. It felt odd to say it, as if I were making it up.

Margot and Chloe will be getting off the bus in a minute, so let me tell you quickly because I'm sure you will be relieved to know that Traci looked better than I expected. Very pale and thin and there are dark circles under her eyes, and a scar at the base of her neck and one on her right cheekbone, and you can tell her ribs hurt when she moves. But she somehow managed to look pretty. She appears to have forgiven Heather for not trying to talk her out of going back to Donny, but that probably has more to do with what a sweet person Traci is than with whether Heather deserves to be forgiven.

Date:   Tuesday, September 1, 10:49 P.M. EDT
From:   SwimSlave
To:     Wanderlust
Subj:   Can't Sleep

I was going to wait until tomorrow morning to finish this. I even went to bed when the kids headed up to their rooms early, tired, I'm sure, from the change in routine. I was almost asleep when Pete came in to the bedroom. I've never really noticed before how much

167

noise he makes when he's pretending to be quiet. He clearly wanted to turn the light on to get himself organized, but instead of just doing it, he just kept sighing and banging into things in the dark. Finally, I sat up in bed. "Oh, are you awake?" he asked.

"I am now."

Pete sighed again. We looked at each other across the bed. "What do you want, Beth. Just tell me what you want."

"I want you to love me. And you don't."

"Yes I do."

We stared at each other for a bit longer, and then Pete leaned over and kissed me. It wasn't the kind of kiss that you give a person you love. It was the kind of kiss you give a person when you want to convince her that you love her, when you're only pretending to love her.

Date:   Wednesday, September 2, 2:57 A.M. EDT
From:   SwimSlave
To:      Wanderlust
Subj:   Of the Heart and Other Parts

I was wide awake after sending my last e-mail so I sat at the computer for awhile, listening to the rain on the roof, and then just for something to do I double clicked on a letter titled *Hot Sex*.

I entered a porn site and watched the graphics unfold, exposing all but a bandaid-shaped rectangle of each body. Looking over my shoulder a bit guiltily, and then pausing for a minute to make sure not a creature was stirring, I figured that as long as I was there, I should look around a little. I found a menu and went through it all item by item, just to get categories. Do you think, in a new relationship at mid-life, that people should try everything, without prejudging it, even if it seems not that appealing or even disgusting, just to have done it once before they're too old? Although I also think it's important to save plenty of time to read poetry to each other, and one can never say enough about the slow sipping of fine wines. . . .

When Heather and I were visiting her, Traci started entertaining us with stories about the famous people she's met at work. They've just finished a rock video for one of Boston's most famous bands. She said they were all so polite and normal, despite their public personas. Traci became friendly with the band's wives who were beautiful and intelligent and nice and came to watch whenever they could. "What's it like?" she asked them one day. "What's the hardest part for you?"

"The underwear," answered one wife. "Whenever the band goes on tour, the fans start up with the underwear again."

"You mean they throw it onstage?" asked Traci.

"Well, of course they do that. That's expected. You can walk away from that. No, they mail the underwear to him, along with the most outrageous notes. Dozens of pairs a week sometimes. Somehow they manage to get them past whatever security measures we take, whatever security we use."

"Wow." Heather cut in to Traci's story at that point. "I've never thought of mailing underwear to anyone. That could be fun." I made a mental note to check all of Pete's incoming mail.

I had a million questions. "Are you talking matching bras and panties or single items? Stuff that you see in the stores or X-rated things? Is the underwear new or has it been, you know, worn? What did the notes say? Did he ever ask you to wear any of it? Did you ever want to keep a piece because you liked it?"

Traci and Heather looked at me as if I wasn't simply asking the questions that anyone would ask, which of course was all I was doing. They looked at me as if I had become sexually unhinged. You don't think I'm becoming sexually unhinged, do you, Thomas?

Can it really be that we'll be together in just a few short days?

Date: Thursday, September 3, 8:35 A.M. EDT
From: SwimSlave

To:     Wanderlust
Subj:   Kids Say the Darndest Things

This morning on the way to swimming, Margot asked, "Are you and Dad going to be all right, Mom?"

Don't worry, honey, I wanted to say. Daddy doesn't love Mommy anymore, but it's okay because Mommy is going to sleep with the neighbor (but never when it will interfere with family life) and then she'll be happy again.

Instead, I said. "We're fine, Margot. Don't worry."

"It's probably hormonal," Chloe chimed in from the back seat. I looked at Chloe in the rearview mirror. With her skimpy cotton T-shirt and tousled blonde curls, she looked more woman than child, far more knowledge-able than a thirteen-year-old should be.

Date:   Friday, September 4, 8:35 A.M. EDT
From:   SwimSlave
To:     Wanderlust
Subj:   Help!

Thomas! There's a rat, a live rat, in the hutch with Rainbow and Star! I don't know what to do! Your timely input would be greatly appreciated.

Date:   Friday, September 4, 9:05 A.M. EDT
From:   SwimSlave

To:     Wanderlust
Subj:   Help, Cont'd!

I didn't mean to scare you before, but I was in mortal terror myself. After I dropped the girls at school and P.J. had gone off on his bus, I decided to walk around the yard and enjoy the morning. Swim season starts tomorrow, and I was thinking that this would be the last morning that my life will be this easy.

I was walking around the yard with my second cup of coffee, noticing how dry the garden looked and thinking I'd turn the sprinkler on in a bit to give everything a soothing soak. I sauntered over to the rabbits' hutch to say "good morning" to Rainbow and Star. Suddenly, I noticed a movement in the corner of the hutch, like a shadow behaving in an unexpected way. And there, at the bunnies' private water bottle, standing on his or her hind legs, and calm as you please, was the most repulsive rat. Not a pet-store rat but a grey-brown street rodent with matted fur and a jagged hairless tail.

I screamed, I'll admit it. And this quite vile and unattractive rat paused and looked at me arrogantly, long yellow teeth bared, as if to say, "Who invited you?" and then calmly turned back to the water bottle. To make matters worse, Rainbow was quietly eating pellets just inches away from the rat, and Star was napping in the far corner. Probably they were terrified but intelligent enough not to give the rat the advantage by showing their fear.

I had no idea what to do, so I backed away on my tip-toes to a safe distance, then turned and ran into the house. My first thought was to write to you, since technically they *are* your rabbits, so that was the point when I sent you my cry for help. I also considered calling Heather but didn't want to give her another opportunity to feel superior.

Gathering my wits about me, I went into P.J.'s room to look for the appropriate weapon. I was all but overwhelmed by the number of choices. My God, he has a regular arsenal in there. I wondered for the first time if all this military stuff was overkill, and then laughed aloud, somewhat maniacally I'll admit, at my pun.

Fortunately, I was able to decide on a toy Uzi with foam bullets. Before I could lose my resolve, I marched back out to the hutch. I hesitated for just a moment in front of the open door, hands trembling, and then, calming myself with my yoga breathing, I took aim and fired repeatedly into the hutch.

I guess I forgot about Rainbow and Star being in there, too. I'm sure my stress level was a factor. Nevertheless, I must accept full responsibility for what happened next. You see, Thomas, I'm afraid that Rainbow and Star haven't known me long enough to trust that the foam bullets were meant only to protect them. I'm sorry to report that, after cowering in the corner of the hutch until my ammunition was spent, they ran off with the rat, who paused from a safe distance to send me a withering look.

I sincerely hope that Rainbow and Star's absence is only temporary and that they will realize eventually that I was only trying to protect the sanctity of their home. Will keep you posted.

Date:  Friday, September 4, 9:13 A.M. EDT
From:  SwimSlave
To:    Wanderlust
Subj:  Not a Clue

No sign yet of Rainbow and Star, nor of their evil rodent leader. I went outside with a flashlight just after dark for a final check before calling off the search for the night. The big dipper was so low in the sky that I had a fidgety urge to push it  up higher and then tuck it in so it would be more comfortable.

Date:  Saturday, September 5, 3:37 A.M. EDT
From:  SwimSlave
To:    Wanderlust
Subj:  In the Night

The clouds must have moved in quickly because I awoke just now to the sound of much-needed rain on my window and I thought of that poem by Edna St. Vincent Millay about the rain being filled with ghosts that tap and sigh and listen for a reply.

Date:   Saturday, September 5, 4:10 P.M. EDT
From:   SwimSlave
To:     Wanderlust
Subj:   Cindi Alert!

Thomas! Cindi is here again! In your house, or at least I assume she is in the house rather than still sitting in her Volvo, which pulled into your driveway about fifty-five minutes ago. I have been watching faithfully ever since, peering through porch screens and raindrops.

Date:   Saturday, September 5, 6:43 P.M. EDT
From:   SwimSlave
To:     Wanderlust
Subj:   More Cindi Alert

Nothing to report other than my diligence. I have left my post only for domestic duties. I would have suggested a cookout, as a ploy to stay out of the kitchen and in sight of your house, but the weather was not cooperating.

Date:   Saturday, September 5, 10:10 P.M. EDT
From:   SwimSlave
To:     Wanderlust
Subj:   And More Cindi Alert

She has the house lit up like she wants to make sure her neighbors know she's there. I hope you are splitting the utility bills. If not, you might want to mention it to the mediator on Wednesday.

Date:  Sunday, September 6, 2:18 A.M. EDT
From:  SwimSlave
To:    Wanderlust
Subj:  Bad Dream

I awoke moments ago, chilled to the bone from a terrible nightmare. I dreamed I forgot my password and couldn't log on to write to you.

Over and over I would type what I hoped would be the magic combination of numbers into the *Enter Password* space. And time and time again, when I clicked once on the *Sign On* space, a notice read, "Invalid password, please re-enter". Try as I might, repeatedly for what seemed like forever, I just could not find a way through to you.

When I awoke, I was clutching the corner of my pillow and squeezing as if it were a computer mouse.

Date:  Sunday, September 6, 11:09 A.M. EDT
From:  SwimSlave
To:    Wanderlust
Subj:  Bagels

I couldn't stand it anymore, Thomas. I simply couldn't stand not knowing what was going on in your house a moment longer. It's not that I'm a busybody, I just want to be able to help you if I can.

So, when I went off on my Sunday bagel-buying ritual this morning, I bought two extras for Cindi and had them put in a separate bag. The weather had cleared and, as I pulled back into my driveway, I noticed that the thirsty soil had already finished drinking up most of the puddles. I thought it only fair to walk into my own house first, to place my family's breakfast in clear sight on the kitchen table, just in case my visit might take longer than I anticipated.

The call of domestic duty answered, I tried for a kind of loose-limbed, casual stride as I covered the short distance from my back to your front door. A quick cleansing breath and then I knocked with what I hoped was neither a threatened nor a threatening cadence.

I guess, in my preoccupation with bagels and approach strategy, I forgot to think about what I would actually say when Cindi answered the door. As a result, when the door swung open with a bit of a groan, I just stood there, wide-eyed and mute. Cindi stared back, deep dark circles under her pale green eyes and a puzzled look on her face. I handed her the bagels, still not able to think of a thing to say. "Thanks. That was nice of you," said Cindi finally.

"You're welcome." Brilliant, Beth.

"So," said Cindi.

"So," I echoed.

We both laughed for lack of a better idea, and we sounded just like Betty and Wilma. Betty Rubble and Wilma Flintstone. I almost said, "Gee, Betty, I wonder where the boys are. . . ."

Of course, I didn't say anything like that. Instead I looked past her at the half-filled cardboard packing boxes scattered around behind her. "Can I help you with anything?" I asked.

"No thanks. I'm all set. Thanks for this, though." Cindi nodded at the white paper bag and I realized that she hadn't even peeked inside.

"They're bagels. Plain bagels. Would you have preferred a flavor? We have cinnamon raisin and sesame at my house."

"No, these are great. Well, I really should get back to work."

Thomas, I'm sorry I wasn't a more successful sleuth. All I know is that she's in there packing and I don't even know if they're her things or not. Maybe she's trying to make off with everything valuable before you arrive, although I don't really think it's my job to try to stop her. Do you?

Just now, replaying the scene in my head, I was happy to notice that it was clearly I who was Wilma. Cindi was definitely Betty. I think that is a breakthrough of some sort for me. Wilma is absolutely the preferred choice. She is stronger, wiser and much more in control of every aspect of her life in Bedrock.

Date:   Sunday, September 6, 4:55 P.M. EDT
From:   SwimSlave
To:     Wanderlust
Subj:   Guess Who's Coming to Dinner?

Guess who is sitting on my porch at this very moment? You are absolutely right. Cindi! I came back from picking up P.J. at a friend's house and there they were, Pete and Cindi, loading boxes into her Volvo. I'll ask Pete if he saw what was in any of them but I'm afraid he was too busy flirting with your soon-to-be-ex-wife to notice.

Oh, the dinner part I referred to above (see Subj:) happened when P.J. and I got out of the car. Pete said, "I was just telling Cindi how she should take a break from packing and join us for a cookout." Smooth, Pete.

So right now she's downstairs sipping wine with Pete while the coals heat up. The phone just rang. It was Maude to tell me that Traci's birthday is next week, and she's planning to have Hans and Biff pick us up in the limos and take us to a restaurant in Boston for a nice dinner/birthday party/"Special Delivery" reunion. I took the phone upstairs under the pretense of getting all the details but really to sneak in and write to you.

Date:   Sunday, September 6, 11:03 P.M. EDT
From:   SwimSlave
To:     Wanderlust
Subj:   G'night

Cindi has just gone home. Don't be angry, but I have to admit that she is really very nice. And not once did she say an unkind thing about you, which I thought was quite classy.

At one point, about to take one of my frequent trips outside to look for the rabbits, I told Cindi the story of their disappearance. Cindi said she was sorry I'd had to get involved, and that they were your responsibility because you brought them home against her wishes. She went next door to get a bottle of wine to share with us. As she uncorked it herself after declining Pete's offer of help, she said that it was a bottle you two had been saving to drink on your 25th anniversary. Apparently you had received a case as a wedding present from her brother and you both decided to hang on to the last bottle for that momentous occasion.

Cindi's eyes were a little teary, so I hope you'll understand that I wasn't going to make her feel worse by refusing a glass. It wasn't the best wine I've ever tasted, or maybe it just didn't age that well. Either way, although I'm sure you're sad about not making it to the anniversary, you shouldn't feel too bad about the wine part.

Date:   Monday, September 7, 10:11 A.M. EDT
From:  SwimSlave
To:      Wanderlust
Subj:   Good Morning

Cindi just came by with a bag of scones and cinnamon rolls for us. They were from a really good bakery, not that we wouldn't have appreciated them anyway.

How is it that I never liked her? I am trying to imagine how she contributed to the breakup of your marriage.

Date:   Tuesday, September 8, 8:45 A.M. EDT
From:  SwimSlave
To:      Wanderlust
Subj:   Swimming Begins Again

I'm just back from my morning swim madness and all three kids are now safely at school. Sorry to be so brief yesterday, but Cindi came with us to a cookout at Heather's, so she could see the goats, and I was too tired to write when we returned.

I didn't know that your older son was in med school. . . .

Heather and I invited Cindi to come with us to Traci's party because we thought it would be good for her to get out and have some fun. She declined, I think with real regret. She said she's leaving right after the mediation.

Date: Tuesday, September 8, 5:30 P.M. EDT
From: SwimSlave
To: Wanderlust
Subj: Oh My God!

I just pulled into my driveway and *your car was in your driveway*. I simply can't deal with this right now, Thomas. But good luck tomorrow.

Date: Wednesday, September 9, 12:09 A.M. EDT
From: SwimSlave
To: Wanderlust
Subj: The Beach

Just before ten o'clock tonight, or I guess technically that would be last night, when the rest of the family was already in bed, still tired from adjusting to the fall schedule, I remembered that the rental movies from the weekend were now overdue at the video store. I walked quietly out to my car, not even glancing at your house. I was hoping hard that you wouldn't hear me. At least I think that's what I was hoping. It could be that I liked this thing between us a lot more when it wasn't so IMMINENT.

I returned the videos, and afterwards I drove to the beach. It was such a beautiful night, warm and dry and lit up by many glittering stars, so I kicked off my shoes and walked down to feel the water. I splashed along, tiny cold waves breaking against my ankles, and then I strolled up to sit in the dry sand away from the water. Grains of sand stuck to my wet feet like socks.

As I sat, I thought about this restlessness that churns inside me a little more insistently every day. I want to be selfish, I want everything to be about *me*—adventure, the excitement of new love—before it's too late. The longing I feel is so unrelenting, as if I exist only to ache for some inexplicable *more*. And here you are, next door at last, in flesh and blood, dangerous and far too real.

Finally, I glanced down at the Day-Glo-green dial of my watch. I was startled to see that it was almost midnight. I pictured Pete tossing and turning in bed, wondering what had become of me. Then I heard the howling of sirens and saw the piercing light of police cruisers. But of course when I returned home, once again not even looking toward your house, even for an instant, my family was asleep. No one noticed I was gone. No one misses me unless they need something.

Date: Thursday, September 10, 8:45 A.M. EDT
From: SwimSlave
To: Wanderlust
Subj: Stunned

Oh, Thomas, stunned is the only word I can think of for what I felt, just five minutes or so ago, upon answering the phone. I was simply not prepared for the deep, husky sound of your voice. It made me think of my favorite Dorothy Parker line, the one about a lover's voice being as intimate as the rustle of sheets.

Unfortunately, thinking of that line made it impossible for me to think of a thing to say to you. I was also having a hard time working around my pounding heart.

And then moments ago I watched from an upstairs window as you drove away to do the errands you mentioned. It is such a relief to know that you're not going away forever. And it is almost beyond belief that we are actually going to see each other tonight. I think you are right in being cautious and suggesting that we meet at a restaurant out of town. And I won't forget to bring the painters' estimates with me.

Date: Thursday, September 10, 9:45 A.M. EDT
From: SwimSlave
To: Wanderlust
Subj: A Suggestion

I think if we run across each other outside later, we should speak casually and act as if nothing is going on. It will look more natural that way. Better than pretending not to see each other.

Date: Thursday, September 10, 9:48 A.M. EDT
From: SwimSlave
To: Wanderlust
Subj: Never Mind

Please ignore last note. I'm overthinking this.

Date: Thursday, September 10, 10:28 A.M. EDT
From: SwimSlave
To: Wanderlust
Subj: And One More Thing

Remember how I asked you to pick me up at the library parking lot so we could ride to the restaurant together in your car? Well, I don't think that's a good idea after all. I mean, what if someone sees my car there and then looks for me inside the library and I'm not there? Or worse, what if one of my kids remembers a last-minute research report and can't find anything on the Internet, and Pete takes her to the library and they see my car and I'm not inside?

So I'll just have to drive, too. But I don't know where it is, so how about if we meet at the library? Whoever gets there first will just sit in the car until the other one gets there and we'll just nod casually when we see each other and then I'll follow you to the restaurant. Okay?

Don't worry. I'm just a little nervous. By the way, how dressy is the restaurant?

Date:  Thursday, September 10, 6:15 P.M. EDT
From:  SwimSlave
To:    Wanderlust
Subj:  FYI

By the way, in case you were wondering, I told Pete I'm going to meet one of my new friends from "Special Delivery" tonight. I just hope he doesn't mention it to Heather, because she'll want to know who, but I think it will be okay because he didn't seem to be listening.

Date:  Friday, September 11, 4:09 A.M. EDT
From:  SwimSlave
To:    Wanderlust
Subj:  Oh, Thomas . . .

I barely slept a wink, I was so busy turning our magical night over and over again in my mind. Did I thank you enough for dinner? I'm sure it was wonderful though I didn't taste a bite. I was feasting upon your nearness.

You know, I had a severe case of cold feet as I stepped out of the car in the restaurant parking lot. I was thinking about how we would have a very nice, chaste dinner. And I would hand you the house painters' estimates. And we would talk. And eat. And I would steer the conversation away from any direction that might be provocative. And then I would just put to rest all of my fantasies involving you. And we could have a nice safe dinner and go home, no worse for the experience.

But the minute I got within smelling distance of you, I felt this strong, physical pull. A chemical response, something olfactory and beyond. You must have strong pheromones because all of my earlier reservations disappeared. I lost all interest in food. In conversation. I wanted sex and I wanted it now. I mean then. I guess I mean then and now.

Please don't take this the wrong way, Thomas. After all the words we've shared, all your e-mail I've read and reread, all my e-mail you've read or at least I think you have read, it was truly wonderful to hear you talk on and on and on. My goodness, all the trips you have taken and the scores of details you still remember about every little part of every single trip. And I am glad you are taking your new travel book assignment so philosophically. I'm sure you'd like your next book to be about somewhere more exotic than Atlantic City, New Jersey but, of course, it's because you did such a superb job on the Laughlin, Nevada, book. I stayed up reading it last night, so I can vouch for your stellar work. I had no idea Laughlin had so much to offer. By the way, thank you so much for letting me look at the galley(s).

But, to tell the truth, I may have missed some of what you were saying, because I was mesmerized by your hands. I kept trying to figure out what held me spellbound: was it your long, tapered fingers, the cute little swirls of hair on your knuckles, the way you gestured airily as you talked and talked? And talked. All I could think about was how delicious it would be to be touched by those hands. Gently at first, and then more insistently.

And, promise you won't be angry, but I kept thinking about that Mary Chapin Carpenter song where she tells the guy about it being so long so just shut up and kiss me.

Once my children are on their way to school, Pete has gone to work, and the coast is clear, I will come knocking at your door, as per the plan we made. I am more than a little nervous, but once you finally kissed me last night in the parking lot, I *knew* that all I really want is you.

See you soon, my love. Is there some other term of endearment you prefer? We should talk about that.

Date: Friday, September 11, 8:45 A.M. EDT
From: SwimSlave

To:     Wanderlust
Subj:   Slight Delay

I'll be there momentarily. Merely making some last minute wardrobe decisions.

Date:   Friday, September 11, 9:05 A.M. EDT
From:   SwimSlave
To:     Wanderlust
Subj:   This, Too

Just a small problem. It's the bed. Or the idea of the bed. I simply can't see making love with you in a bed where you've done it with Cindi. I mean, I really like Cindi and I'm just not sure I could handle it.

I had a crazy thought, just now, to call that toll-free mattress number they advertise on the radio, 1-800-DIAL-A-MATTRESS, although that can't be right because it has too many digits. But, it would take too long to get one delivered, and what would we do with it afterwards—just leave it out by the main road, and hope that no one would notice?

You don't happen to have a guest room you've never had sex in, do you?

All right. I know I'm stalling. I'll be there in a minute.

Maybe I'll take a warm bubble bath first. Okay, half an hour.

Date: Saturday, September 12, 8:13 A.M. EDT
From: SwimSlave
To: Wanderlust
Subj: Hmm . . .

As I sit sipping my morning coffee on the porch while P.J. watches cartoons inside and Pete and the girls speed up the highway toward morning swim practice, I glance out the porch door and see a rose lying on the stoop.

A single red rose. Nice, but definitely from my garden. It's a variety called Blaze, known for its blood red flowers and powerful scent, as well as its brutal, piercing thorns.

And I know it's from you, Thomas. I picture you waiting for the sound of Pete's car pulling out of the driveway. I watch you tiptoe across our property line, enter my flower garden, look around to see what there is to take.

I'm still processing the events of not quite twenty-four hours ago, as if there might still be a way to make them fit, if only I can think long and hard enough about it. I just need to find the key puzzle piece and then all the rest of the pieces will have a place to go.

It started so well. I can see you clearly in your dark paisley silk robe as you opened the door. I can do this, I thought, as I joined you at the kitchen table for a cup of coffee. I *want* to do this.

And then the sound of a static-y radio from outside your house. I couldn't believe you invited the house painters over to start their work when you knew I would be there. I have to live in this town, remember? I thought you'd be more discreet than to try to kiss me with men on ladders leaning up against your house. Sorry I left so abruptly, the sight of those painters was hardly an aphrodisiac.

I guess I thought that extramarital sex would be a little more romantic. No offense, Thomas, but so far it doesn't seem to be worth rotting in hell for. And I'm pretty sure that if we stop right here, then technically I haven't even been unfaithful. So we had a couple of pretty good kisses, it could happen to anyone. And I, at least, remained fully clothed. I think I can still wrap my monogamy around me like a cloak of slightly tarnished armor. After all, it's not as if technically there has been any real sex, or even that much pleasure.

But then I remember how long I've wanted you and wonder if we should give it another chance. I mean, everybody has a bad day now and then. And you are such a great kisser. Plus, I bought the best lingerie, from "Victoria's Secret", and you never even got to see it.

Thank you for calling all those times yesterday. As I sat there not answering the phone, I knew it was you even before you hung up instead of talking to the answering machine. I read your multiple e-mail(s), too. It was very nice to finally get more than an occasional response.

I think perhaps, Thomas, that this wasn't such a great idea after all, and to continue any further along the road toward actually having sex would be to follow the path of least integrity. And then the next minute I think we should just keep trying until we get it right. I mean, what an unsatisfactory final memory.

Pete will be back with the girls before long, and then tonight I'm going out for Traci's birthday. Let's give it some time, and see if an answer makes itself known.

Date:   Saturday, September 12, 10:22 P.M. EDT
From:  SwimSlave
To:      Wanderlust
Subj:   Holy Moly!

What the hell are you doing in my house, Thomas? I was so shocked after Hans pulled the limo into my driveway a few minutes ago. I jumped out and Heather followed, because she had driven her car here first, supposedly to make one less stop for Hans, although I knew it was really because she wanted to see Pete. Everybody knows that Heather only thinks of Heather. Anyway, when we heard voices on the porch, I never expected one to be yours. Oh my God!!!!!

And what am I doing writing to you if you're downstairs?

I will send this now, although I'm not sure why. Then I will flush the toilet. See, I'm functioning well even though I'm quite rattled.

Did you tell Pete anything? Anything at all about us?

Date:   Sunday, September 13, 1:05 A.M. EDT
From:   SwimSlave
To:     Wanderlust
Subj:   Relieved

You just left. Thank you for walking Heather out to her car. What a perfectly casual way for you to leave, so much better than trying to arrange a moment alone with me. I don't think Pete suspected a thing.

That wasn't so bad, once I got past the initial shock. It was, however, otherworldly to walk in and find you and Pete sitting next to each other in matching wicker porch chairs, surrounded by a ring of empty beer bottles. Heather managed somehow to appear to give her eager and exclusive attention to you both when she asked, "So what nice things have you been saying about me to your friend, Pete?"

And it was so kind of you, Thomas, to give so much of your attention to Heather, especially since you'd never met. It really helped me to relax when you didn't spend your time giving me steamy glances. Pete didn't seem the least bit suspicious, either. In fact, he didn't seem to be watching me at all, so I know you didn't say anything, not that I really thought you would have. But still, it was a relief.

At one point I looked over at Pete, and he was watching Heather flirt with you. He had the saddest look on his face. A look of disappointment that almost made me regret every wanton and lascivious impulse I've felt towards you.

Time to sleep. How about if I stop by with bagels in the morning, because I don't think it would arouse suspicion now that you're a friend of the family. We can talk and . . .

. . . whatever.

Date:   Sunday, September 13, 4:01 A.M. EDT
From:  SwimSlave
To:      Wanderlust
Subj:   ??????

I don't know what made me go to the window when I awoke a few moments ago. Some instinct. Some inkling. Some whisper of passion that floated across the night air and into my window.

I can't fucking believe that Heather's car is still in my driveway.

Date: Sunday, September 13, 4:08 A.M. EDT
From: SwimSlave
To: Wanderlust
Subj: ?????

Did I overreact to the painters being at your house? Was that it? You know, Heather's probably had lots and lots of affairs, if half of what she says is true. She might have picked up anything from anyone.

Date: Sunday, September 13, 4:21 A.M. EDT
From: SwimSlave
To: Wanderlust
Subj: ????

I know it would be really immature if I went out to Heather's car and started beeping the horn. I also know it would not lead to anything positive. Still, I'm going to do it anyway because I can't think of anything else to do. So I am apologizing in advance for the scene I am about to cause.

Date: Sunday, September 13, 4:32 A.M. EDT
From: SwimSlave
To: Wanderlust
Subj: ???

I just went out to see if Heather's car was locked. It was. Then I wandered over to your house to see if I could see anything through the windows. I couldn't, although I did see that one of the upstairs rooms has a light shining in it. I bet it is your bedroom. It seems as if Heather doesn't have a used mattress phobia.

On the way back to my house, a good thing happened. Even in the worst situations, there's always some good. Rainbow and Star were back in their hutch, munching away happily on pellets. They seem to have ditched the rat. I knew they'd come to their senses.

Date: Sunday, September 13, 4:39 A.M. EDT
From: SwimSlave
To: Wanderlust
Subj: ??

You know, I figured out something while the "Special Delivery" group dined and shared stories at the restaurant. My friends and I have all experienced our dea incessu patuits, even those of us who can't pin down an exact moment of revelation. We've become the goddesses of doing exactly what we want to do.

After dinner we moved to the lounge to listen to a singer. A blues singer who has been around since the old days, but never really made it, never quite became famous. I can't even remember his name but I could tell he understood about love.

And I found myself imagining what it would be like to lie on a bed surrounded by satin pillows, dozens of them, while a lover touched and teased every inch of me with his mouth and hands and penis. When I couldn't stand it any longer, he would finally pull my legs around his neck and bring his tongue to just the right place and play me like a finally tuned guitar.

It was great. Thomas. Imagine that, it appears that goddesses have even better fantasies than mere mortals. I couldn't quite tell who the man was though. . . .

Date: Sunday, September 13, 4:58 A.M. EDT
From: SwimSlave
To: Wanderlust
Subj: ?

I am simply too tired to stay awake any longer. I'm sure Pete will be up soon, and when he notices Heather's car, he will take over the vigil. I wonder if he will mention it later, or if we will pretend nothing happened.

I wonder if we will both conclude that we have had enough adventure, and simply *will* ourselves to be in love again. Can one *decide* to be in love with someone based on having been there before?

I plan to sleep late, so that everyone wonders if I might be sick. Maybe they'll wander upstairs by noon, Pete bringing me coffee, one of the kids carrying the Sunday paper. There'll be breakfast on a tray, perhaps with a bouquet of flowers, one that they have every right to pick from our garden. They'll sit on the edge of the bed, ask me if I feel all right. Maybe Pete will lay his hand on my forehead to see if I have a temperature. At the very least, maybe they'll let me sleep for a few hours.

Date: Sunday, September 13, 6:01 A.M. EDT
From: SwimSlave
To: Wanderlust
Subj: Good-bye

I can't sleep, Thomas. I am breathing deeply: four calming counts in through my nose, four cleansing counts out through my mouth, aware that I might possibly be performing this ritual backwards. Is it in through the mouth and out through the nose? Having been to Tibet, you would know, I suppose, and would love to correct me with just the barest hint of superiority, so slight that I couldn't be sure if you are acting superior or if I'm just being overly sensitive.

Too late. I am calm now, calmer than I have been in a couple of months and some small change of weeks and days and hours. Calmly I will continue while I still have time before Pete and the kids wake up. These, Thomas, are my final words: 1) Feed your own goddamn rabbits: take at least this finite responsibility for your life. They have enough food to live on for about a week, but you know Rainbow will try to eat her share plus Star's. 2) While you're at it, take in your own fucking mail and 3) deal with your own goddamn fucking lawn service.

I *am* breathing deeply: four calming breaths in through my mouth (just in case), four cleansing breaths out through my nose. No ... I think it felt better the other way.

I see that your car is gone now. Heather's too. I hope you at least are gone for good. When and if you come back to your house, if you have to tie up loose ends yourself, assuming you can't make Heather your next ... what's the word I'm looking for ... oh, there it is—sucker. If that doesn't work and you have to return, don't even look at my house, don't glance at the windows, don't peek at the garage to see if my car is there.

Just one more thing. Right now I'm hearing that old Carly Simon song playing in my head, and you really *are* so vain that I bet you think this was all about you. I know you'll find it impossible to believe, you'll think I'm just trying to save face, but all of this was only about me. You were merely convenient, barely more. You were an ear, a pair of eyes, the mirror I needed to gaze into until I could see myself naked.

You did me a big favor, Thomas. So consider this letter my parting gift, my thank you for services rendered. I feel so much better for getting all this mid-life restlessness out. And now I'll take one more deep breath in, and let it all go. After I've caught up on my sleep, I'll invite my family out to dinner, somewhere with good food and a view of the ocean. And we'll take plenty of time to enjoy each other's company.

And soon I'm going to have a pajama party. I'll invite Millie and Maude, Traci and Kate, Alex and Helen, Mary Paige and Betsy. I think I'll invite Heather, too, although I'm not at all sure if it's only to pump her for the prurient details of her most recent adventure. We'll sleep out in tents in the woods for old times' sake, and I'll get up early to see the sun rise.